Feet of Clay

Feet of Clay

Sheila Morgan

y lolfa

With my love and grateful thanks to my husband and daughters for all their help, patience and encouragement.

First impression: 2012

Cover design: Sion Ilar
Cover photograph: Gelli Colliery (1965) by Glyn Davies,
by permission of Rhondda Cynon Taf Libraries & iStockphoto.

ISBN: 978 1 84771 4244

Published and printed in Wales
on paper from well maintained forests by
Y Lolfa Cyf., Talybont, Ceredigion SY24 5HE
e-mail ylolfa@ylolfa.com
website www.ylolfa.com
tel 01970 832 304
fax 832 782

CHAPTER 1

Rapid Changes

FRIDAY, JUNE 13TH, 1952. Carrie Thomas, lying awake, lifted her head off her pillow to look at the alarm clock. It was too dark to see it, despite the street lamp shining dimly through the curtains. She reached out her arm and felt for the switch on the little table lamp, glanced at the clock and switched it off again. Half past six! She moaned to herself. If she got up now, what would she do with herself for the next couple of hours? Yet if she stayed where she was, the fidgets would start and she'd end up waking Albert. She turned her head to look at him, her eyes now getting accustomed to the dark. He was fast asleep, bless him, snoring gently beside her. Her face softened as she watched him. *Aw, my ol' love,* she said quietly to herself, thinking again about all they had lived through during their marriage: the poverty and hardships – near starvation on times – two world wars and the crippling effect the first one had left on her husband during his voluntary service; and then the terrible, unbearable tragedy of losing two of their beloved children during the second. The impact of that on Albert had been horrendous, bringing him to the very edge of a complete nervous breakdown. Thank God for baby Glyn's timely arrival. It had saved them both, she knew. They had come through it all, thanks to that little one and with each other's support, ending up closer now than they had ever been – more honest and open with each other, able to talk about any worries, their feelings and doubts, not shutting off and moithering about things.

She had her sister and her brother-in-law too, to thank for that, for their intervention and help at that crucial time. Carrie caught her breath, remembering. It had all happened in the few days leading up to Doris's funeral. What would they have done without Martha and Joe then? And in the years that followed? Those two and her youngest daughter, Ivy. Oh, she was so glad Ivy, Jim and their two girls had stayed in Crymceynon. And Vera, after little Glyn's birth. She always referred to Vera as her daughter-in-law, despite the fact that her son, Glyn, had been killed before they could marry. In fact, she was more like a daughter. Ivy looked on her like a sister, too. Not that Vera could ever take Doris's place. Doris's place was safe and secure, right here in her heart.

She glanced across at Albert again. He was looking old, love him. It had all left its mark on him. They were both on their way to seventy now and him still working at the pit. Not underground anymore, thank goodness, but still grafting hard. He was afternoons today. How many more years did they have together, she wondered. She turned onto her side again. Oh, it was no good! Once she started mulling over things, her mind flitting from one thing to another, she may as well get up, washed and dressed and mull over them downstairs. She eased herself slowly out of the bed, fished for her slippers with her feet and tiptoed out onto the landing, closing the door quietly behind her. She padded softly towards the smallest back bedroom which had recently been transformed into a bathroom, thanks to her son-in-law and his pals.

This morning, as on every morning since its installation, she caught her breath as she entered, her eyes running over the dazzling white porcelain of the toilet, the wash-up and the bath. Oh! Who would have thought she would have ended up in such luxury in her lifetime! To be able to lie full length, in a bath of warm water that could be warmed up again at the turn of a tap whenever she felt like it, totally relaxed and comfortable – just like a baby must feel in its mother's womb, thought Carrie, smiling to herself.

This morning, she contented herself with a good wash. She didn't want to wake Albert with the noise of the water running. Never again would she have to boil buckets of water on the fire and keep two kettles simmering on the hobs for doing her weekly wash or for Albert's daily bath to remove the pit grime. Never, ever again! Mind, she hadn't had to get the old tin bath in for Albert for quite a while now, not since the nationalisation of the pits in 1947. Showers had been installed in them. Now, he went to work in clean clothes and came home in clean clothes, his dirty pit clothes carried home in a carrier bag. And what a difference that had made to her life, too!

Sunday was Albert's day for a good old soak. The showers were efficient but you had to be quick as there was always someone waiting to take your place. Every Sunday now, he followed the same ritual routine: one o'clock, dinner; two till three-thirty, a nice little nap in his armchair by the fire; four to five-thirty, a bit of tea and a browse through the *Sunday Express* and then his bath. Carrie could say goodbye to him for at least three-quarters of an hour for that. He was as clean getting into the bath as he was getting out of it but what did it matter, so long as he enjoyed it! Sometimes, if she had to go upstairs for something, she could hear him humming or singing his favourite hymns to himself as he did his ablutions. It brought tears to her eyes.

Carrie made her way downstairs and into the parlour to open the curtains. It was a lovely day out there, the sun just rising over the mountain, shining brightly. She stretched herself while she took in the view, feeling her 'bag of old bones' sorting themselves out. Pity to waste a morning like this. She would slip out for an hour or two, take a walk over to lower Crymceynon to Parson's the butcher's to see if he had any lambs' hearts. Or perhaps a breast of lamb. She looked at the grandfather clock in the corner. She would have to go early, be first in the queue. Just gone seven. Her mind ran over what she would need. There was enough stale bread in the breadbin for the stuffing, she knew, and a cabbage on the stone in the pantry that Albert had picked from the allotments yesterday and plenty of carrots, parsnips or swede to choose from, stored in the garden shed, together with a sack of potatoes. Oh, and mint sauce! Albert must have his mint sauce with lamb, no matter what cut it was or how it was cooked. There was plenty of that in the back garden. Right then, that was dinner sorted.

She walked to the kitchen, wondering if the fire would still be in. There was no chill in the air to greet her as she opened the door. She might be lucky now! Albert had banked it up with damp, small coal as usual, before they went to bed and more often than not, with a bit of encouragement, it could be coaxed into life again the following morning. The high, old-fashioned iron grate was now replaced by a new Foresight enamelled, pale mustard-coloured cooking range with a neat, tiled, fawn-coloured surround and hearth. The fire was set down low on one side with two ovens on the other: a large one on the bottom for her main cooking (and a damn good cooker it was, too!) with a smaller one above, which came in very handy for her milk puddings, rising the dough for her bread, keeping Albert's dinners warm and drying sticks to light the fire with.

Carrie put out her hand and touched the oven doors. Mm.

They were still warm. Lifting the small, metal blower from the alcove by the grate, she placed it in position over the front of the fire and held a sheet of the *Daily Herald* over it. The sudden draught sucked the paper to the metal and around it, like a skin. By the time Carrie had made herself a pot of tea, boiling the kettle on the gas-stove, the paper had started to scorch and a red glow shone out from below. Yes, it was in. Good. Quickly, she snatched the paper down, folded it and used it to remove the hot blower, taking it outside to cool down. She gave the bottom of the grate a gentle riddle with the poker, added a few small nuggets of coal to the now brightly burning fire, swilled her hands and sat back with a contented sigh, into her comfy armchair with her china cup and saucer in her hands. *A lady of leisure, that's what I am these days*, she told herself, lifting the cup to her lips and savouring both the tea and the difference these alterations had brought to her life. This was all down to Vera who'd had the foresight to buy 2 Duke Street with some of the money she'd inherited from her father. It would be a good investment for her sons, but Carrie and Albert had been assured that it was theirs at the same rent until the end of their days.

Jim, Tom Pierce and Billy Griffiths hadn't been long doing all the alterations. Since the end of the war, they had set up a nice little lucrative business between them, doing hobbles (odd jobs) in their spare time whenever they could and the more they did, the more efficient they became and the more efficient they became the more word got about and the more demand increased. Everyone seemed to be at it these days, Carrie mused – modernising, as they called it. Ivy's house and Vera's were a picture: carpets everywhere, a washing machine each, a refrigerator – Jim even had a small van now! Well, it was a necessity really, she supposed, what with the business taking them farther and farther afield. They were doing so well that Jim was seriously thinking of packing in the pit and devoting his full time to it. There just weren't enough hours in the day for him. He was teaching Vera's two grown-up sons to drive now. They'd be the next to have their own transport, and good luck to them. Well, there was plenty of money going into that house now, what with both boys employed in the pit and Vera able to take in more sewing now that little Glyn had started school. Our Ivy wasn't short of a bob or two either, with her wages as cook in the two schools coming in, Jim's wages and the profits from his hobbles firm. Though since Pauline had gone to Cardiff University that, of course, had been an extra expense but she'd nearly finished there now. Carrie's mind switched courses again.

University! The first in the family to get there, as far as she knew, unless you counted our Martha's husband. He had spent years in London, training to be a doctor. That was when he had met and fallen in love with Martha. She was working in Lyon's Corner House then and he had called there regularly. They say opposites attract, well that certainly happened with those two! Whereas Joe was quiet, reserved, a bit on the shy side, Martha was full of life, outgoing, jovial. But it was a good match, a very happy marriage despite the fact they had been unable to have children. Such a shame that, they would have made wonderful parents.

Her thoughts returned to her eldest granddaughter. She was glad that nice young boy from the Navigation was at the same university, for Pauline to have company amongst all those strangers. She wondered if romance would blossom there in the future? You never know. She could do worse. Pauline was 'doing' Welsh and history, intending to become a teacher. Carrie had forgotten most of the Welsh she had known and it was lovely whenever Pauline came home and chatted to her in her native tongue, bringing it all back again. It wasn't spoken much in the village now and hadn't been for many years thanks to the 'knot' of long ago being tied too tightly and loosened too late. It was Jim who had first aroused his daughter's interest in the language, when they were little, Carrie remembered. He didn't know much Welsh himself but, being a proud Welshman, he had taught them both to say the Lord's Prayer: *Ein Tad, yr hwn wyt yn y nefoedd*; all the verses of the national anthem: *Mae hen wlad fy nhadau*; the correct translation of a 'box of matches' – which few people knew or used – *blwch o fflychiau* – and to rattle off the whole of Llanfairpwll... without a mistake! Both girls had loved rolling their tongues around it all.

Carrie paused in her reminiscences and looked up at the clock on the mantelpiece. Just gone quarter to eight. It was too early to go out just yet, the butcher's didn't open until nine o'clock. She looked around her. There was absolutely nothing she could get on with. She had emptied the little ashpan, banked up the fire with some small coal in case she was a bit late coming home and had cleaned the vegetables. There was no washing to be done – she had done their 'smalls' yesterday and Ivy had taken her sheets and towels over to do, insisting on it again.

"They're no trouble in the twintub, Mam! I just have to put them in and take them out, practically and they're washed, rinsed and spun dry. Wet sheets are too heavy for you to struggle with now, so take telling, leave them to me and that's an order!"

"But Ivy bach," she had said, "you've got enough to do what with your housework and your job."

"Ma-am!"

"Alright, alright. Thanks Ivy, love."

There was no ironing waiting in the clothes basket either, not that that was a chore anymore with an electric iron these days. And she had dusted right through only yesterday. Carrie wasn't used to this – time on her hands. It took a bit of adjusting to. She got up and strolled to the passage to see if the paper had come and to pick up her milk bottles from the doorstep. Yes, they were both there. She closed the door as quietly as she could, put the bottles on the stone in the pantry and went back to her chair to open the paper and read the headlines. She noticed the date in the top corner – Friday, June 13th. Oh. Carrie was inclined to be a bit superstitious about some things, like spilling salt, breaking a mirror, walking under ladders – and Fridays that fell on the thirteenth of the month! She shook her head.

Oh, don't be so daft! she scolded herself, crossly. What was the worst thing that could happen? That Gilbert Parson didn't have any hearts and that she had wasted her time walking over there, that's all. Besides, she could call at the 'Cop' while she was there. She was out of flour and one or two other heavy things: pop, Spel washing powder, dried peas, brown sauce and tinned pilchards. She would catch the early delivery and she could have a nice little chat with Margaret Pierce. She had been serving in the Cop now for five years and had told Carrie that she loved working there. Carrie was glad to hear that as it was through her that Margaret had got the job. She had been there the day Wilfred Williams, the manager, had mentioned that one of his staff was leaving to have a baby.

"Well, if you're looking for a replacement Wilf, I know of a very nice girl and a damned good worker, who's leaving school this term."

And that was all of five years ago! How time flew these

days. She had never told Margaret that she had stuck her nose in and had recommended her and had instructed Wilf not to, either.

Ten minutes to eight. Five more minutes and she would go. From always having too much to do, now suddenly there was not enough, thought Carrie, restless. All or nothing. People will never be satisfied, will they? She rose her eyebrows at the fickleness of folk, including herself. The look faded and her eyebrows descended into a worried frown as her train of thought veered off in yet another direction.

Yes, there was a distinct air of dissatisfaction in the air somehow, seeping through the whole village these days. A desperate rush about things. Not like it used to be at all. Carrie tried to sort it all out into words. It was like a kind of hunger, she decided, for changes, money, clothes, posessions and as soon as one 'meal' was over, people were looking for the next. The younger generation, in particular, seemed prone to it. It gave her a slightly uncomfortable feeling thinking about it, finding it vaguely worrying and unsettling and she didn't like it. Where would it end? Everyone seemed to be in a race to beat his neighbour in 'bettering' themselves. Life was never like that before. Money and its acquisition were all people seemed to talk about nowadays, the chief topic of conversation, and with lots of women still in employment there was quite a lot of it floating about in some homes. Carrie had a sneaky feeling no good would come out of it if it wasn't handled carefully. Snippets of conversation she had heard while out shopping flitted through her mind.

"Have you been in Joan Davies's house lately? That paper on her parlour wall cost nearly a £1 a roll, I was told!"

The response had voiced some bitchiness.

"Oh, trust her!"

Then again: "I'm sick of hearing about the Pritchards and their bloody caravan in Porthcawl."

"As if she's ever been used to holidays!" whispered one to another.

And again: "Rosemary Jones has just had a bathroom put in. A pink one, for goodness sake! It must have cost her something!" And where had she got the money from, her tone had implied.

Mm. Superiority, one-upmanship, jealousy, thought Carrie, shaking her head. Not nice qualities to have. She shuddered a little, then shrugged.

"No, don't be daft!" she told herself, crossly. "It's just human nature for goodness sake!"

After a lifetime of deprivation, downright misery and hopelessness, this was the first opportunity most people like them had ever had to enjoy some of the good things in life. At long last. It would soon settle down. You couldn't blame people for wanting to better themselves, for wanting more out of life. And they were prepared to work damned hard for it, most of them, after all. Fruits of one's labour. What was wrong with that? The old attitudes and standards were still there, underneath, she was sure of that. Besides, it wasn't her place to judge others, was it? Not when she herself had willingly taken her share of it.

She got her basket, her Cop book and her purse from the pantry, her coat from behind the kitchen door and left the house. A nice long walk on a beautiful morning like this would soon put everything back into perspective.

CHAPTER 2

The Parson Household

BEHIND THE MAIN street of lower Crymceynon and a little higher up the valley side was Fair View, a row of large, semi-detached houses with big bay-windows. In number fifteen and almost directly behind their butcher's shop, lived the Parson family – mother, father and son. It was an impressive house with a big garden, front and back, covered by lawns and bordered by flowering shrubs and perennial plants. The large grained and varnished door opened onto a porch, its walls decorated to halfway with large Victorian tiles. The porch door and the panels on either side were glass from halfway up with a big star pattern cut into the centre of each large pane and edged with narrow panes of royal-blue and ruby-red stained glass. It opened onto a square hallway and long passage, the staircase rising on the right and two doors leading to the parlour and middle-room on the left. At the end of the passage was the kitchen door, a replica of the one in the porch. Small tiles of different colours and laid in an attractive, almost Arabic design, covered the whole of the floor of this area. Both of the shut-off rooms were nicely furnished with old but good quality furniture. They were rarely used. Upstairs were three large bedrooms and a bathroom which had been installed when the house was built. Mr Parson had inherited the house from his parents. Mrs Parson kept it immaculate. Very few changes had been made. Esther and Gilbert had now lived here as husband and wife for nearly twenty-two years. Esther thought the world of her husband – she adored him.

Never, in her wildest dreams, did she ever think she would marry one day, let alone bear a son, her beautiful, precious, handsome Godfrey!

It was Friday, June 13th, seven o'clock in the morning and Esther was, as usual, the first to be up and about. She was nearly sixty-two but still a good-looking woman, slight and neatly shaped, her thick, mousey hair, now peppered and streaked with grey, plaited and wound up into a bun that sat on the top of her head, making her look taller than her five-foot-four inches. Her eyes were a greyish green, large and dark-lashed, her nose small and slightly upturned. Even, white teeth, just visible when she talked, formed two neat rows behind full but not over-fleshy lips. Her mouth turned up naturally at the corners giving her face a permanently happy expression. She carried her age well, looking at least five years younger than she was, though wearing little make-up. She was dressed smartly in a pale grey, pencil-slim skirt and pale pink, hand-knitted twinset. Her whole appearance gave one the impression that she was fully content with her lot in life. And she was – up to a point.

Today was her son's birthday. The big one, the special one, his twenty-first, his coming of age. Oh, she was so proud of him. No-one could ever have borne a better son, in nature and appearance. He was nearly six feet tall, straight and smart, with thick wavy hair, several shades lighter than hers, wide-set eyes more blue than green, a straight masculine nose – just like his father's – and a strong, square jaw with a deep cleft in its centre. A veritable Greek God, an Adonis.

Her mind went back to the day he was born. She hadn't been even the slightest bit nervous when her contractions started, despite it being her first child and she being nearly forty-one years old. What a wonderful experience it had all been, giving birth to him. She honestly had not noticed the pain, eager and desperate as she was to see her child. And the second she saw him, she idolised him, naming him Godfrey there and then, quickly shortening it to God, her little God. And God he had been ever since, the 'little' being dropped as he grew.

Esther had only been married to Gilbert for nine months before the baby's arrival. Just the marriage itself had changed her whole outlook on life and her hopes for her future. She hadn't dared hope for anything more. She had known him since they were children, had grown up together and she was always totally at ease in his company. He was the one – and the most important – of the very few people she had ever been able to feel at ease with. His friendship had helped her through all her very difficult school days and had grown between them as the years went by, her fondness for him developing into love as she developed into womanhood. She felt – she knew – that it was reciprocated but no move was made by him in that direction and she sensed his restraint, a holding back in him, as the years went by, one after another. Still, she valued his company and his friendship and lived in hope. Maybe one day. Time passed but at least he showed no interest in any other woman. Knowing instinctively that he did love her, she concluded the only reason that could be holding him back, was 'it'. Not her personally but 'it' – the terrible affliction that always hovered, that could never be got rid of. It was perfectly understandable to her. She just had to accept it, be thankful for small mercies and grateful for his affection.

Gilbert, like his father before him, was a butcher, a businessman, or would be after his father's days. He would need a wife he could take out and show off at get-togethers, meetings and dinners with all the other tradespeople, someone who would be an asset to the business, his parents advised him, knowing of his fondness for 'that girl', and making it clear without actually mentioning her, that they didn't approve of his choice. What good would someone like her be at such functions, they thought, even if she could be persuaded to attend? Someone born with such a debilitating handicap – a vicious stammer that could send her whole head into jaw-thrusting, jerking spasms that could last for long, agonisingly painful seconds as she fought and struggled to force out the words through tightly-clenched teeth.

All her life Esther had withdrawn from people as much as possible as a result of her affliction, except those closest to her, finding it far less stressful to remain cocooned in her own environment than venture out and suffer unnecessarily. Strangely, it rarely happened in the company of those chosen few, arising only when she was worried or upset or excited about something. Marrying Gilbert, straight after the demise of his parents, had been her salvation, had opened the door for her to a near-normal life. He had always been able to separate the 'it' from the woman and she loved and respected him all the more for that. And now, here she was, after nearly twenty-two years of married bliss.

She was in the middle of cooking breakfast for her two men when Gilbert walked up behind her. He put his arms around her, turned her towards him and kissed her firmly and fully on the lips.

"Morning, my love."

She slid her arm around his neck and kissed him back just as fully.

"Morning, Gil."

"Today's the day, then? Twenty-one, eh? Seems just like a year ago he was in napkins, learning to walk and talk, doesn't it? A little scrap of a lad. Look at him now, eh?"

Esther loosened her arms from around his neck and gently pushed his shoulders back so she could look at his face.

"Thanks Gil, for everything," she said suddenly, tears welling in her eyes.

"No. Thank you, Est. For being my wife, for giving me our son, our lovely, wonderful son," he whispered in her ear.

He had never regretted even one day of the years they had been together. It should have been longer, much longer, thought Gilbert guiltily as he sat by the fire to glance through the paper and sip his first cup of tea of the day. All those years wasted. They could have had more children. Still, they had Godfrey and no-one could wish for a better son. Everyone spoke highly of him, everyone liked him – always polite, always pleasant and smiling, always ready to give a helping hand. Twenty-one! It was time he started thinking of getting married himself now, settling down, raising a family. Grandchildren! Now there was something to look forward to, eh?

Gilbert nodded his head with resolve – whatever girl he chose would meet with Esther's and his approval. They wouldn't stand in his way, not like his own parents had done. They had never liked Esther, they had made that obvious. Pressure was put on him in all sorts of subtle ways. But it had only made him all the more determined that he would have her one day. He had loved his parents, despite their prejudice and interference and, being an only child, had felt torn between wanting Esther and pleasing them.

So he had put off marrying her but had kept on seeing her and would wait. If he couldn't have her with his parents' blessing then he wouldn't have anyone, no matter how hard they tried to fix it. Waiting had been hard to do. He couldn't tell Esther why, he couldn't say that he wanted desperately to make her his wife but that his parents didn't like her. Words like that were best unsaid. Sometimes, looking back, he regretted not being more of a man perhaps, and standing up to them. But the past was past and Esther had proved to be well worth waiting for.

Upstairs, Godfrey, bathed and dressed, stood before the full-length mirror in his wardrobe door, looking at his reflection as he tied his tie, a look of satisfaction on his face as his eyes swept over the tall, athletic build of his image.

God, you're a handsome bugger! he told himself with a wry grin. *You could charm a robin off a starch box with those good looks!*

And he did attract the girls. But the girls around the village were not the ones he wanted. He wanted someone classy, stunning, experienced, who liked to live life at a pace, enjoying the good things in life as he did. Or would do, if he had the cash! That type of girl and all that went with her cost money. And he didn't have any. Well, not as much as he would like, as much as he needed. His expression changed to a look of anger and frustration. The feeling mounted in him as he combed his hair. *But your time will come, God,* he told himself. *It won't be long now. Bide your time and act your part and your time will come.* He turned and left the room, thinking as he descended the stairs, about the reception awaiting him. There would be a card, handed over by his mother, and his father would stretch out a closed fist that probably held two five-pound notes, with the words: "Don't spend it all at once now, lad!" – meant as a joke but with a serious undertone to his voice. Well, here goes.

"Ah, here he is," said his father, rising from his chair as Godfrey entered the kitchen. "Our birthday boy – oops! Sorry, son – our birthday man!"

They both laughed as Gilbert put his arm around his shoulder and slapped his back.

"Happy birthday, son!"

His mother stood near, waiting her turn, then stood on tiptoe to plant a kiss on his cheek, all sorts of emotions and memories rising in her.

"Many happy returns of the day, G..G..G.."

Damn! It had to happen now, today of all days. Her head jerked violently, her pretty mouth distorted and went into spasms as she desperately fought to control it. Godfrey reached out and put his arms around her, gently stroking her back, smiling sympathetically but thinking as he did so: *Here we go again! You stupid, silly-looking woman!*

Gilbert had returned to his armchair. He knew from experience the less fuss that was made, the quicker she recovered her composure. The stroking calmed her and the involuntary, thrusting convulsions gradually slowed, then stopped. She was too excited, that was the trouble. There, it had passed. She took a deep breath and looked up at her son, apologetically, something deep inside her telling her that he always hated these spasms and had little patience with them. He couldn't help it, love him. Most people reacted the same.

"Sorry, God." She smiled but there was shame in her face. "Happy birthday, son!"

He bent and kissed her, affection written all over him. If anyone could fake sincerity, he could, when necessary. She handed him his card. He opened it and read the inscription – 'To our loving, perfect son, with all our love, Mam and Dad xxxx'.

"Aw, thanks Mam," he said, kissing the bun on the top of her head, then again, "Thanks Dad," as he walked to the mantelpiece to stand the card on display.

His father looked up from his seat and held out his fist, nudging him in the stomach with it.

"Here's a couple of quid, God, for you to be going on with."

Godfrey opened his hand to see what had been thrust into it. Three five-pound notes! Hmm, more than he had expected, then!

"Don't go mad now and spend it all at once!" chuckled his father, adding "A fool and his money are soon parted, mind!"

Godfrey chuckled too, pretending to join in the joke.

"But let's be serious for a minute, son. That money I've just given you, from your mother and me, is to spend with your pals to celebrate your birthday."

Thanks for your permission, Dad, thought Godfrey.

"But what do you really want, eh? Now that you've reached manhood?"

You wouldn't want to know, thought Godfrey but the temptation to tease and aggravate his father was too much. He would wind him up, just for devilment to see what he would say.

"Well, a nice little Austin Seven wouldn't go amiss, Dad!"

Wait for it!

"A car!" said his father, his voice full of derision. "What the hell do you want a bloody car for?"

That's for me to know and you to worry about.

"You don't go out that much!"

Exactly, you're right there, Dad.

"And when you do, you go in one of your mates' cars."

Right again, Dad.

"And you've got the van. You know you're welcome to the van whenever you want it, after work, son."

Oh, right! And that would draw the girls alright, wouldn't it? Just like a magnet, emblazoned as it is with 'Parson and Son, Purveyors of Quality Meat, Established 1870'.

"A car indeed!"

Godfrey's face broke into a wide grin. He had achieved his goal.

"Only joking, Dad!" he said, holding back the satisfied guffaw that was threatening to burst out of his mouth. But his father wasn't quite so sure.

"Aye, I should think so, too. No, I'm serious, son. About our business, now. My father founded it, I've built it up and now it's your turn, to modernise it, go with the times, bring it up to date. I want to know what your plans are, where you want it to go from here."

Esther was carrying their hot plates of bacon, sausages, eggs and fried bread to the table.

"Right," said Gilbert, getting up and moving to the table. "Breakfast is ready. Have a think about what I've said, what you want to do, what plans you have for the future and we'll have a chat about it tonight. And we'll see about sorting out some cash for you to get it all started. Right, boy?"

He slapped his back. His son nodded as if considering all this seriously.

"Good lad! Now, let's get stuck in while it's warm. Friday is our busiest day, after all and goodness knows when we will have time for the next meal or a cuppa."

Godfrey did just that, glad to give his facial muscles, cramped with the continuous smiling, something else to work on. His father's words stuck in his mind. The business, always the business! Plans to expand it? It brought in enough as it was. All work and no play? No way! He wasn't his father. He had other ambitions. Yes, the shop was doing alright as it was and had done all through the war years even. Especially through the war years! Nothing at all had gone to waste during those years. Every scrap of offal, off ration, had been snapped up. He had seen his mother counting the takings every evening and balancing the books. And the bags of money that were banked weekly. Well, he wanted some of that. What else was money for? And he wanted it now and by God, he intended getting it. Ha! The irony of what he had just said dawned on him. Yes, God was going to get it, alright! All of it and before very much longer.

The business was the be-all and end-all of his parents' lives. And what did they get out of it? His father's only indulgence was two ounces of pipe tobacco, bought every Friday morning to last for the week. And his mother? She got all her pleasure from looking through and buying from catalogues, spending hours browsing through them, picking out clothes for them all, shoes, things for the house and whatever else took her fancy. Oh, and they both looked forward to and enjoyed a glass of whisky each, of an evening. Just the one. Even that was bought wholesale, by the boxful, to save money. Godfrey had had it up to his neck about the scrimping and saving, "watching the pennies and the pounds looking after themselves" and "thrift being a hard lesson to learn when you are young but once learned, would stand you in good stead for the future". His father would have made a bloody good preacher. Huh! He had the right name for it, too – Parson!

I'm twenty-one for God's sake! he raged to himself. *My life is galloping on and what have I done? Where have I been? Nothing, nowhere!*

Not until his National Service and boy! – was that an eye-opener to what was out there in the big, wide world. He had played his cards right from the word 'go'. One of his NCOs had advised him that if he sent an allowance home out of his weekly 28 shillings then if something should happen to him, his parents could claim a pension for him. Godfrey knew that by doing so it would appeal to his parents, that they would appreciate his thoughtfulness and would over-reciprocate. Subsequently, letters from home regularly contained a sheet of postage stamps (which could always be sold) or a ten bob or a pound note. He also soon discovered that a good supply of coffee, bought while on leave, was also an excellent boost to his income. On entering the army he had been assigned to the catering corps, having had experience of butchery in civilian life, which gave him access to the stores – another lucrative little source of income! His posting was Germany, where anything could buy everything, and he had complete freedom to go anywhere on his time off. He soon pal-ed up with two other boys of the same ilk and tastes as himself, the three of them preferring to spend whatever leave they had in London rather than their home towns. Great times were had in 'dens of iniquity' – casinos, nightclubs, pubs and other places of ill repute. It was a crash course in education and it whetted his appetite for more. If he could guarantee that he wouldn't be posted to somewhere dangerous, he would have signed on!

He had been home about six months now, straight back behind the counter in his father's butcher's shop, just like it was before – same hours for the same wages and suffering the same routine. And what did his father have mapped out for him! More years of exactly the same.

"All this will be yours one day, son. After our days. You will probably be getting married in the not too distant future, eh? And start a family, have responsibilities. You'll see the sense of it all then."

Get married? Have a family? Not if he could bloody-well help it, he wouldn't. He wanted to live his own life by and for himself, not to be told what to do by anybody, not to have to care for anybody, be responsible for anybody. After their days? They could live forever the way they were going. They were in their sixties now. They probably had another twenty, twenty-five years to go, maybe even more! He would be middle-aged, still having done nothing, gone nowhere and, perish the thought, still living at home. No, that was not going to happen.

He pushed his now empty plate to one side, reached for his side plate and some toast and buttered it, spooning out some marmalade as his mother poured him another cup of tea.

Gilbert's mind too, had been racing while he ate. His son was in for the shock of his life tonight! For years, he and his father before him had kept a secret stash of sovereigns in the house, adding to them whenever they could. Banks shouldn't know all your business. Best to keep something up your sleeve. Over the years, they had mounted up into quite a considerable sum, their value increasing as the years passed. The hiding place for this valuable horde was in the *cwtch* under the stairs but no burglar would ever find them. They were inserted in neat rows in the gaps between the steps and risers of the staircase, a row on each step for as high as could be reached; the first ten steps, each one containing twenty of the gold coins. Two hundred of the beauties. A month ago, Gilbert had put the last one in place. No-one, not even Esther, knew of their existence. It didn't do to tell women everything, either. And he would ensure that Godfrey wouldn't tell her – Esther loved to slip her son a fiver now and again, thinking he didn't know. He wouldn't deprive her of that pleasure.

When war had broken out, he had been in two minds as to whether to bank them or not, but had decided against it. A staircase, apparently, was the strongest construction in a house, the last thing to collapse. That was why people were advised to shelter in there during an air-raid. Besides, if Britain was invaded, then a ready supply of gold would come in very handy. Gilbert had always taken time to work out all the pros and cons of anything to do with money. It paid out in the long run. None of your spur-of-the-moment decisions for him! They would remove all of the sovereigns tonight while Esther was upstairs having her Friday night shampoo. He looked forward to it.

CHAPTER 3

Her Secret Love

FRIDAY, JUNE 13TH. It was a quarter to seven and Margaret Pierce was already up and busy, putting the house to rights before she went to work. It would be a long day today, Friday. The lower Crymceynon branch of the Co-operative Wholesale Society opened half an hour earlier, at half past eight and closed at half past six, an hour later than the rest of the week. Most customers shopped for their rations and big orders on Fridays, stocking up for the weekend. The shop would be noisy with chatter and choc-a-bloc most of the day. The staff would be lucky to snatch a tea-break in the morning or the afternoon. Ah well, she would have an early night tonight and it was half-day tomorrow.

Her parents were still in bed, so too was what was left of their brood: Brian, the twins and her youngest sister. The other six were long gone, married and some with families of their own, now. At twenty years of age, Margaret was a slim, dark-haired, beautiful young woman, though she was totally unaware of the fact. She moved with a natural grace, her body toned to perfection by all the hard work she had done throughout her young life: helping her mother, keeping the house clean and tending to the younger ones. Her nature was that of her mother's in that she was popular with everyone but there the similarity between them ended. Having borne all those children, Elsie-May had given in early in life, her energy rapidly declining, swallowed up by continuous pregnancies and her genuine love and care for her husband and brood, leaving nothing to spare for herself or the house. She had put on weight with her increasingly sedentary lifestyle and now her health was seriously failing. Arthritis plagued her, resulting in a vicious circle of less movement, more weight, greater pain. It broke Margaret's heart to see her suffer. Whatever she could do to make her mother's life easier, she would, finding the time and the energy to do so, somehow.

The house was much nicer and easier to run these days, thank goodness. Her father was bringing home good money now, what with his wages from the pit and the money he earned from his hobbles after work. And Brian was a big help, too. For the last couple of years he had taken over his father's allotments and looked after his mother's chickens, putting in a few hours every day after school, to begin with and now, after his shift in the pit. He was allowed to keep a good share of the profits from both ventures to save towards a longed-for motorbike.

Each member of the Hobbles Firm, as Margaret liked to call her Dad's and his mates' business venture, now owned their own houses which were the first to be converted. All three men: Jim Edwards, Billy Griffiths and her Dad had quickly become expert and proficient at cementing, plastering, wiring, plumbing and woodwork, gleaning information from mates in the trades or from library books. The more they did, the easier it got. It was an absolute pleasure keeping the house clean these days, thought Margaret, as she unwound the lead from the Hoover to give the three downstairs rooms a quick going-over. Tiles now covered their kitchen floor and oilcloth and carpet squares in the other two. There was less dust to settle since the Foresight grate had been installed, as there were no ashes to rise, just a small pan to be emptied and no more blackleading to do – no more Zebo stains on her hands, under her nails, ever again – Hallelujah! Her chores finished, she looked around with proud satisfaction. Clean and shining. And it would stay like that for the whole weekend!

It was nearly eight o'clock, time for her to leave for work – there was quite a long walk to get there. Brian would see to the younger ones and get them ready for school. She set off, walking with a light, quick pace, her thoughts occupied with the day ahead of her. She was quite excited – as always on a Friday. She would see *him* again. He came into the shop, regular as clockwork at ten minutes to nine for his father's pipe tobacco every Friday morning. She might even get to serve him. It seemed to fall to her more and more often as time went on. Sarah and Joan would suddenly be busy and unavailable to serve. She blushed thinking about it. They guessed she liked him, they teased her to bits about him. But he showed no sign of any interest in her. As far as he was concerned, she was just another member of staff. She was a victim of unrequited love.

It had been love at first sight for her. That very first week, when Godfrey Parson had stepped into the shop, the sunlight bright behind him. She had stopped in her tracks, stunned by this vision before her. She had read about that sort of thing in magazine stories, never dreaming it could actually happen. She remembered him vaguely from her school days but she hadn't taken much notice of him then. He was in a class above her, their paths rarely crossed. He certainly had an impact on her now. Since that first sight of him as a man, she had looked forward eagerly to every Friday morning but at the same time dreading them, nervous in his presence.

Reaching Parry's Terrace, on her way to work, she spotted Carrie Thomas a few yards ahead and increased her speed to catch up with her. Mrs Thomas had always been one of her favourite people. Mr Williams, her manager, had told her in confidence that it was thanks to her that she had got the job, that Carrie had highly recommended her but not to let on that she knew. It didn't surprise her, knowing Carrie. Mr Williams had called to her house on the very day she had finished school and asked her if she would be interested in the job. She had started work the following Monday and had loved every day there since, at the Co-operative Wholesale Society, known by the majority of its customers, she had quickly discovered, as the Cop, by the English immigrants as the Co-op and by the *crachach* (the posh people) as the Quorp!

It was the hub of the village where everyone caught up with the news, local and global; where young mothers-to-be were given hints on confinement and child rearing; where jokes were cracked and sometimes tears were shed; recipes swopped, advice given on how to cure different ailments; where and what job vacancies there were; who was courting who, who was getting married and who had died, and general gossip indulged in. All things to all people and never a dull moment, thought Margaret.

"Morning, Mrs Thomas," she said, catching up with Carrie. "Lovely morning, isn't it?" she added, though it would have been lovely to her if it had been thundering and lightning and blowing a gale. All Friday mornings were lovely mornings.

"Oh, Margaret! Good morning, love. Yes and it's a pity to waste it so I'm off to your premises. I've run out of flour and yeast and a few other things. Thought I'd come early, then I'll catch the delivery van, save me carrying anything. I might as well order a case of pop, too. Albert's always thirsty since he had the job in the stoke house!"

Carrie had paused to chat, then suddenly realised she was holding Margaret up. She would be late.

"Oh, don't let me keep you love," she said hurriedly, patting her arm. "You go on. My old legs don't go as fast as they used to. You go on, don't mind me. I'll take my time."

"Give me your book and your order then, and I'll put it up ready for you and keep it on one side in case you remember something else when you call in and have a look around."

"Oh, would you? Oh, that's kind. I can pop over to Parson's then for some lambs' hearts, if he's got some, and I'll be home early to make the stuffing."

She handed over her list and book. "Thanks, love."

"It's no trouble. Bye, Mrs Thomas."

That girl was a treasure. Carrie had always said she would never have to look for work – work would come looking for her! It wouldn't be long before some bloke came looking for her, too, and snapped her up. Carrie hoped it would be someone who would appreciate her, treat her right.

Margaret walked quickly on, turning to wave and smile back at Carrie as she turned into the long street.

CHAPTER 4

The Cop

MARGARET REACHED THE Cop at a quarter past eight. It was one of the few shops in the street that hadn't been built for the purpose. It was one of three, big, double-fronted houses that had existed before proper shops, specifically built, had sprung up on either side and opposite. It was in a bad state when she had first started working there. Now it was on its last legs and there was talk of demolition and a move to new, modern premises in the very near future. That would be nice, thought Margaret, but how far away would it be? Would Godfrey still call in for his father's tobacco? She had quite an affection for this old place despite its state and the hard work needed to keep it clean. She had had a lot of fun here with both the staff and the customers. The bell ting-ed as she opened the door. Moira, the cashier, was already there in her room to the right, sitting at her desk counting bags full of bread and milk checks and stacking them in little piles.

"Morning, Moir."

"Morning, Maggs." She motioned to the window. "And a nice one too, for a Friday, thank goodness. I hate wet Fridays."

"Mm, and me. When the shop fills up you can see the steam rising off them all!" Moira laughed.

"You're right and one or two of 'em don't smell too sweet either!"

"No. Evening in Paris it isn't, is it!" She turned towards her left and walked through the shop itself to the room behind to hang up her coat and deposit her bag, shouting as she went: "I'll give you a hand with all those checks now, Moir."

"Ta, Maggs."

Moira's wages were a bit higher than those of the other girls but she certainly earned them, thought Margaret. She would roll up her sleeves and join them in the sweeping, scrubbing, shelf-stacking and window cleaning whenever she had a spare moment. No job was beneath her. She even took her turn cleaning the toilet.

"Why shouldn't I?" she replied when they protested. "I use it, don't I?"

So they all reciprocated whenever they could, by straightening book slips and helping with the endless check counting.

Wilfred, the manager, was in the back room breaking up slats from an empty orange crate to get a fire going in there. The old house could be cold even on the warmest day. They had a gas ring to boil their kettle on but it was nice to sit in front of a fire to drink their tea.

"Morning, Mr Williams."

Only Moira was allowed to call him Wilf and then only in the absence of customers. It was an unwritten – and unspoken – rule of etiquette. The two of them had worked together for years. He was a short little man, in his late fifties, white haired, pink-skinned and with the bluest of blue eyes Margaret had ever seen. A confirmed bachelor, he had lodgings with a woman in town and had lived there for the last ten years or so, since acquiring the post of branch manager in lower Crymceynon. His landlady, coincidentally a Mrs Williams, spoiled him rotten, doing all his ironing, washing and cooking, supplying all his needs. A good wife in all but licence, reckoned some of his customers. He, in turn, spoiled her, keeping her supplied with a regular bagful of any little treats that were still scarce or on ration, courtesy of the CWS. A perfect partnership. So why should he want to get married, remarked his customers. As things were, he got all of the pleasures of married life – with none of the pain!

Wilfred Williams, Margaret had soon discovered, was a many-faceted, many-talented man when dealing with his customers. When necessary, he could turn into a financial adviser (usually in the weeks leading up to the end of the quarter, when all books had to be cleared of debt!); a tender-hearted good listener or a shoulder to cry on; sometimes, even a money lender if someone was in dire straits; a peacemaker, a great diplomat – a psychiatrist even, on occasion! His one pet hate was waste. Very little was ever thrown out from the Cop; cracked eggs were sold off cheap, as were broken biscuits, rusty tins or broken packages and there was always a grateful customer waiting: beneficial to those and to the profit margin. It was joked that lower Crymceynon branch made the profit of three. But in all the five years that Margaret had now worked there, she had never heard a bad word said against him.

As she joined Moira, she wondered how many others were as happy and contented in their jobs as she was. The work was physically demanding, being on your feet all day and humping heavy crates, sacks, boxes and sides of bacon about but the great majority of the customers were lovely, some of them real characters who could put you in stitches. She woke every morning, looking forward to the day ahead.

Oh, and that first Christmas! And every one since. What a shock that had been! The generosity of them all, even the ones that could least afford it. It all came as a complete surprise. As every member paid their books, they left either a small gift (often a handmade one) or a tip for each of the girls with Moira, who distributed them during the last hour on Christmas Eve before the shop closed. Margaret had gone home laden with gifts and the equivalent of more than a week's pay in tips!

Sarah, the first hand, and Joan, the other assistant, arrived. They lived in the same village lower down the valley and travelled to work by bus. They looked an odd couple side by side. Sarah was tall and angular with fair, coarse hair, including eyelashes, eyebrows and a faint moustache, which all glistened in the sunlight, and she had a ruddy complexion. Joan, on the other hand, was short, rounded, dark-haired and pale-skinned. She was a bit of a hypochondriac but suffered genuinely from asthma and a very weak bladder. But to be fair, she pulled her weight despite both conditions. Sarah was married and had been for over a year now, but had no intention of starting a family, she said, until she had saved up a nice little nest-egg. Joan was courting strong – an engagement was on the horizon.

The checks all counted, Margaret set about putting up Carrie's order while the other two unpacked a large block of butter and began weighing it into ration portions. They all chatted as they worked.

"How did it go last night, then?" Margaret asked Joan. Derek, her boyfriend, had invited her home to meet his parents.

"Don't ask!" said Joan.

"Why? What happened? Tell us!"

"Oh, they were very nice, his Mam and Dad, very welcoming."

"But?"

"His mother kept on plying me with tea. I had a cup

when I arrived, another with my meal and another a bit later. I had to ask to go to the toilet three times!"

"Well, there's nothing wrong with that, you daft thing."

"Yes, but I wanted to go again before I left. By the time we'd walked to the bus stop I was busting."

"Mm," said Sarah drily. "And it was raining and we all know what affect that has on you, don't we?"

"It was piddling down!" They all burst out laughing. "There was nowhere I could go and the bus due any minute."

"How did you manage?"

"Well, I knew I wouldn't last out until my stop..."

"You didn't!"

"What else could I do?" Moira had come in just in time to hear the end of her story.

"I don't think Derek noticed, what with the rain and everything. He never said anything!"

They all shrieked.

"Well, he wouldn't have, would he, you daft 'aporth!"

Wilf came in from the back room.

"Enough of this banter now, girls. It's Friday, mind."

They resumed their work for a few minutes, but could never stop chatting for long when the shop was empty. Moira, stacking the portions of butter in the glass-fronted provisions counter, started them off again. She addressed Sarah. "What goodies have you brought for lunch today, then, Sar? Come on, tell us, whet our appetites!"

Sarah's sandwich fillings had to be seen (but not tasted) to be believed. Whatever had been left after their meal the previous night was usually incorporated between rounds of bread the following day. Waste not, want not. Unperturbed, Sarah had a think.

"Um, swede and sprouts mashed, with a touch of HP sauce for starters and stewed apples and custard for afters!"

"You're joking! You haven't! Stewed apple and custard, in a sandwich?"

"I have. What's wrong with that?"

"What's wrong with it? What's right with it!"

The girls were often near to hysterics with her combinations.

"Listen," said Sarah, seeking to justify her odd choices, "if you've got a dish of apple and custard for your tea, you like a slice of bread and butter with it, don't you? Well, what's the difference? And anyway, it's not so runny when it goes cold!"

Every day was like that, thought Margaret, holding her sides. It was a pleasure to come to work. They all got on so well together and made a good team. She finished putting Carrie's order together and was packing it into a cardboard box just as Carrie entered the shop. It was twelve minutes to nine.

CHAPTER 5

Comparisons

"WELL, COME ON, son," said Gilbert, rising from the table. "It's nearly half past eight and I've a side of pork to start jointing up before we open. Birthday or no birthday, special or no, there's work to be done and money to be earned!"

"Ready when you are, Dad," said Godfrey cheerfully and putting on his jacket. They left the house, walked to the end of the street and turned down the little hill that led to the lane behind the shops. During the walk they said little to each other, as was normal, the business of the day ahead now occupying Gilbert's mind. They stopped at the bottom of the hill to pass the time of day with Mr Charlie Bowen, owner of the baker and confectioner shop a few doors up from their own. He was on his way home after the night's baking. He looked tired out. His wife would now be serving in the shop for the rest of the day – and maybe his son Dudley – if he had a mind to.

Greetings exchanged, the two older men started to discuss some business.

"I'll go on, Dad, and get all the trays laid out ready, is it? And pop over the Cop to fetch your tobacco."

"Aye fine, son. If you would, then. I'll be there now."

"Bye, Mr Bowen."

"Bye, Godfrey. Oh, and many happy returns of the day!"

He looked at Gilbert as Godfrey walked away and jerked his head backwards. "You've got a good lad there, Gil." There was envy and a tiredness in his voice.

"Aye," said Gilbert, beaming with pride, "And don't I know it!"

The sight of Mr Bowen had only served to heighten Godfrey's anger. Now there was a man who knew how to treat a son, he told himself, jealousy and resentment surging through him. Dudley, who was about the same age as himself, had everything. Always had. Showing off with his proper cricket bat, ball and stumps down at the pavilion in the park, when they were just kids! At fourteen, he'd had a brand new Phillips Roadster bike to ride up and down the streets on, the girls all shouting after him: "Give us a ride, Dud!" Then a few years later, for his eighteenth birthday, a BSA 500cc motor cycle. Godfrey would have given his eye-teeth for one of those. His latest acquisition, a few weeks ago for his twenty-first, what did he have? Only a bloody car, a Morris Minor! He and some of the lads had already been to Blackpool in it for a holiday. A holiday – what was that? Godfrey had never been away from the village until his calling-up papers had come. His days were all fully booked with the business day in, day out; week in, week out; year in, year out, ever since he had left school. The butchery opened at nine and closed at six every day except Wednesday and Saturday when they shut shop at one. No customers to serve on those afternoons, but not afternoons off, by any means. There was still plenty of work to be done. Saturdays were the worst. For the last few months, it had been his job to do the rounds, driving the van to the more remote streets, delivering, selling and collecting debts. He rarely finished before seven o'clock and where could you go then? All his friends were already out enjoying themselves at the new coffee bars and jazz clubs in town. When he had mentioned this to his father, all he got was another sermon.

"Money mounts slowly through graft, son, but soon melts away through play. Believe me – I've seen it happen more than once. That damned fool of a boy Dudley Bowen, now he'll go through that business of his father's like a hot knife through butter once he gets his hands on it. You mark my words. I would advise you not to get too friendly with him. He'd lead you astray if he could, but thank God, you've got more sense than that wastrel. I don't need to tell you that though, do I son?"

Godfrey had shaken his head and agreed.

"All I want," continued his father, "is to see you settled before I die with a nice wife and children of your own. Now there's riches for you, eh?"

Huh, he could whistle on that score, thought Godfrey. He wasn't going to get tied down, not for years yet, if ever. All work and no bloody play wouldn't be much fun, would it? He wanted a taste of all that was out there. He clenched his teeth.

"No, I want more than just a taste. I want to gorge myself on it, all of it, get my fill of it. I want to live, with a capital 'L' and to do that I need money. Now!" He banged the trays about in his frustration as he got them sorted ready for the different joints of pork.

Gilbert and Charlie Bowen parted company and Gilbert continued on his way to the shop. Aye, Charlie was right about our Godfrey. Jealous, that's what he was. You could hear it in his voice and see it in his face and with good cause, poor beggar. That son of his was turning out to be a right good-for-nothing from what he had heard. Never satisfied, always wanting more. Gilbert didn't know what was happening to some of the youth of today. There was just no getting through to some of them. Words like responsibility, duty, respect, obligation – all seemed to have disappeared from their vocabulary, all of a sudden. Why couldn't Dudley be more like Godfrey? Where had Charlie and his missus gone wrong? Some daughters were the same, some kids just wouldn't take telling for their own good anymore. Parents' authority was being whittled away. Thank God for his Godfrey, that's all he could say!

Chapter 6

Poor Godfrey

Godfrey, dressed in his dirty, blood-stained overall from yesterday, kept an eye on his father, busy sharpening the wide-bladed knife, ready to slice through the side of pork hanging in the coldroom. The blade being drawn expertly and rapidly up and down the steel would be razor sharp for a neat, straight cut. Gilbert paused and examined the edge once more. It was to his satisfaction. He placed the steel and the other implements to one side of the huge chopping block and walked into the cold room. Godfrey followed behind. His father stood in front of the side of pork, holding on to it at his shoulder level with his left hand. With the knife in his right hand, he began to slice through the meat.

The knife was sliding smoothly through the carcass when Godfrey came up behind him. It took a split second to place his hands over his father's, left over left, right over right and force them towards each other. As the knife sliced swiftly through the last few inches of the side of pork, then straight into his father's neck, Godfrey pushed him forward and jumped back, away from the gush of blood. Quickly, he removed his overall, rolled it up and placed it in the bucket of cold water that held yesterday's soiled meat cloths then put on a clean one, checking his face and hair for any blood splashes in a small mirror placed strategically on the wall to reflect the shop area. Walking casually to the back door he slid the bolt across, locking it, entered the shop and left by the front door, locking that too behind him. His total composure surprised him and he felt very confident and pleased with himself as he pocketed the keys and crossed the road to the Cop. He glanced at his wristwatch on the way. It was exactly ten minutes to nine.

Margaret Pierce had just finished serving Carrie Thomas with a couple of extra items to her order. Also in the shop was Mrs Lewis-the-Post, an attractive, flirtatious woman in her late thirties who was being served by Sarah. Confident of her looks, Mrs Lewis loved to draw attention to herself – to be in the limelight. Her dyed blonde hair hung in loose curls around her shoulders, her forty-inch bust was hoisted to nearly chin level and her make-up carefully applied (this, early in the morning, thought Carrie, disgusted). She turned as the shop bell ting-ed, a welcome smile spreading across her face as Godfrey entered.

"Morning, ladies!" he said with a beaming smile.

They all looked round at him, smiling back.

"Morning, birthday boy!" said Mrs Lewis, seductively, adding to the others "It's his twenty-first today, isn't it Godfrey?"

There was a chorus of "Oh, many happy returns of the day!"

"Now how did you know that?" he scolded Mrs Lewis, wagging his finger at her.

"Your father told me," she replied, moving and patting his arm. "You're the apple of his eye, you are!" She reached up and plonked a kiss on his cheek as if she was giving him a very special, privileged present. "Happy birthday!"

Godfrey's eyes swept over the other women, the two girls behind the counter smirking behind their hands and Carrie tutting openly. Mrs Lewis relished the company of men, especially young, handsome, fit ones. She liked to tease and flirt but would have run a mile if they had responded with serious intent, everyone knew. For devilment, Godfrey put his arm around her, bent her backwards slightly and plonked one back on her cheek.

"Thank you, Mrs Lewis, that's made my day, that has!"

"Oh!" she fluttered, putting her hand up to her face and waving it about like a fan. "It's a good job my husband isn't here to see that, Godfrey Parson. He'd have your guts for garters!"

Silly little madam, thought Carrie, tutting again, she thought she was God's gift to men. She lost patience with looking at her and turned to Godfrey rolling her eyes upwards, sympathising with him at the woman's ridiculous behaviour.

"Is Dad over in the shop, Godfrey?"

"Aye, he's there, early as usual. He's jointing a side of pork. At least, that's what he said he was going to do. I've just popped over for his tobacco. He'll want a cuppa and a pipeful when he's finished. It's hard work humping all that meat around. But will he let me have a go? Will he, heck!"

"Oh, he will from now on, I bet."

"Well, I know how to do it. I've watched him often enough and I did my share of it in the army, in the catering corps."

"Mm," said Carrie, "it's an art, is butchery, I always think, and he's so quick at it, isn't he? I've watched him, fascinated, when I've asked him to bone a breast of lamb or something. Those knives of his are lethal!"

"Oh aye, and he will have them sharp."

Carrie turned to Margaret.

"Serve Godfrey, Marg. I think I've had all I want now. I'll just have a last look around while I wait for Godfrey to open up."

Margaret looked up enquiringly to him.

"Uh, the usual please, Maggs. Two ounces of Franklyn's Strong pipe tobacco."

He had called her by her name! He had never done that before. She smiled at him shyly and reached into a drawer below the counter, taking out two red and white packets and placing them on the counter before him. She looked up at him again, waiting patiently.

"Uh, that's all thanks."

They both waited now, looking at each other.

After a few seconds Margaret, chuckling a little, said: "Your book, then? For me to enter them?"

"Oh, sorry." He delved into his pockets searching hurriedly, keeping his eyes on her face. He made a show of going through them all in his overall and trousers then raised his empty hands and shrugged his shoulders. "I've forgotten it!"

Sarah, standing close by and busy serving Mrs Lewis, bumped purposefully into her as she turned to take a tin of peas from the fixture behind her, winking as Margaret turned and scowled at her.

"Er, shall I pop over and fetch it or pay for it?"

"No, don't pay, you'll lose your dividend on it. I can put it on the counter book for you till you come in next. Don't worry, it doesn't matter."

She opened the drawer and took out a big book, found the page and entered the item, knowing his book number by heart. He still stood there.

"Er, I could bring it over later. What time do you close?"

"Half past six on Fridays."

"And what are you doing then? Going anywhere nice?"

She glanced at Sarah who was humming a little tune under her breath and grinning as she entered goods into Mrs Lewis' book. Carrie, strolling around, looking at the shelves was also watching, listening and enjoying this little conversation. He was going to ask her out! Well! Now wouldn't those two make a nice pair! Two very likeable, very popular, nice youngsters. A good match. The look of approval on Carrie's face did not go unnoticed by Godfrey. He was feeling omnipotent by now. Little did she know what lay in store for her in the next few minutes when she came over to the shop!

"Tonight?" said Margaret, flummoxed and in answer to his question. "No, not tonight. I thought I'd have an early night tonight."

Sarah had ducked down behind the counter and was tugging at the hem of her overall. Distracted by this Margaret, without looking down, snatched it free and moved slowly out of her reach.

"Oh, that won't do! Friday nights are the start of the weekend." He paused, looking at her then added "Fancy going to the pictures?"

Sarah had moved too, and disappeared below the counter again to resume the tugging. Margaret glanced down to see she was grinning from ear to ear and nodding her head vigorously. She snatched free again, looked up at Godfrey and was lost for words.

"Oh, um…"

Sarah got up suddenly.

"Ooo, Maggs, Fred Astaire and Ginger Rogers are in the Palace!" She looked at Godfrey. "She loves their films, don't you Maggs?"

Margaret looked daggers at her.

"Right then! I'll see you at six-thirty."

Margaret panicked. She hadn't expected any of this and was totally unprepared to deal with it.

"But I'll have to go home first!"

"That's alright. I'll walk up with you and we can walk back down the canal bank. It will be quicker that way."

He knew where she lived: he had seen her on his rounds and had watched her surreptitiously as she stretched to clean the parlour window or scrub the front step, thinking she looked a bit of alright. For just a bit of fun, nothing serious though. She wasn't what he was after. He wanted someone with a bit of panache, sophistication, someone who knew her way around. He had noticed her hesitation and added quickly: "I'll wait for you by Lowe's shop, if that's alright."

There was no way he wanted to meet her parents. She needn't worry on that score. Margaret breathed out a sigh of relief. She had been worried about just walking in with him in tow without warning or preparing her parents first. It wouldn't be fair to them. She nodded once or twice, trying not to appear too keen at this proposal.

"Oh, well, yes, alright then."

There were silent smiles all round, including Wilfred, who now stood at the provisions counter slicing bacon on the machine. Godfrey looked at his watch again.

"Right, ladies. It's nine o'clock and the butcher's is open for those that want it. Bye, Maggs, see you later."

"Bye," she whispered shyly. She knew that she would always remember this moment, this day, Friday, June 13th. It would be burned into her memory. The day her life took a new turning. And she relished the thought.

The two customers and Godfrey crossed the road, Godfrey in front with Carrie close behind him just in case 'fancy pants' wanted lambs' hearts too, and Mrs Lewis bringing up the rear. When they reached the door, he took his time fishing for the keys in his pocket and selecting the right one to open up, chatting casually to his two customers as he did so. On entering, he turned the 'closed' sign to 'open', lifted the blinds, opened the counter gap, put his father's tobacco by the scale on the counter and perched a pencil behind his ear.

"Right then, ladies, which one of you is first?"

"Me, I think," said Carrie, glancing at Mrs Lewis and daring her to disagree.

"Right then, Mrs Thomas. What can I get you?"

"Have you got any lambs' hearts, Godfrey? I thought we'd have stuffed hearts for dinner today. Albert does love 'em." She remembered to cross her fingers, the date being what it was!

"You spoil that old man of yours! I'll give Dad a shout." He turned his head and moved a few steps towards the door behind him and yelled "Dad? Dad! Any hearts left? Lambs' ones?"

There was no answer.

"He's probably slipped to the lavatory. I'll go and look now. Anything I can get you while I'm in there, Mrs Lewis?"

"I'd like some liver, if you've got some please. Lambs'. It must be lambs'. We don't like pigs'." She turned to Carrie. "Pigs' livers have a much stronger flavour, don't they? We don't like those." She wrinkled her nose. Carrie nodded, not wanting to get into any conversation with her if she could help it. Godfrey nodded.

"Right then. Two lambs' hearts and some liver," looking at Mrs Lewis, smiling and adding, "lambs' only". He turned and went through the door.

This was it, now, this was the moment. He had to see it

through. He knew he could do it, he had to – there was no going back. *Keep calm, don't get excited, take your time, keep in control.* He called out "Dad!" once or twice as he went in, waited a second or two, then screamed in an agonised voice: "Dad! Oh, my God! Dad! No! Oh no!" His voice lowering now, he let out a heart-rending moan. "Help, someone! Help me, please!" and sank to his knees beside the body just as the two women, following the sound of his voice, appeared by the door of the cold-room.

The horrendous scene before them brought them both to an abrupt halt, their minds trying to register what they saw. Gilbert Parson lay face down on what looked like a very large piece of meat. Pools of thick, dark blood had spread and soaked into and around the top half of his body, covering the meat beneath him and the floor around him. His right hand, just visible by his left shoulder, still held a wide-bladed knife that was deeply embedded in his throat.

Carrie, feeling sick and faint, leaned against the door-post. A flash of what her daughter Doris must have looked like, when she was found after that air-raid with shrapnel embedded in her throat, swirled around her head. On the verge of losing consciousness, she was saved by her maternal instinct. Godfrey, his hands hovering and wavering above his father's body, seemed about to lift him in his arms.

"No!" she said quickly, moving involuntarily to his side, "Don't touch him, love! Best not to."

She took his hands in hers and called to Mrs Lewis to give her a hand to lift him to his feet. Godfrey was limp with sobbing. Together, they walked him slowly out of the cold-room, one on either side of him and sat him in one of the armchairs in the backroom where he and his father sat for their tea-breaks.

"Put the kettle on the gas-ring, Mrs Lewis, and make a strong pot of tea for us all, with plenty of sugar." The woman was all of a dither. "And pull yourself together, for goodness sake! I can't cope with everything by myself!"

Mrs Lewis took some deep breaths and did her best to comply.

"I'm going to lock the front door. We don't want anyone wandering in on this. And I'd better phone for a doctor or somebody to come. Do you know who their doctor is?"

Mrs Lewis nodded, glad that she was of some use. "Yes, Dr Tilsbury."

"Have you got his phone number?"

"Yes. It's in my bag, somewhere."

"Get it while I lock up."

Carrie went through to the shop. Thank goodness there was no-one about yet. She looked by the scale on the counter. Yes, the keys were there alongside the tobacco. Quickly, she locked the door, turned the sign to 'closed' again and pulled down the blinds. Next she looked around for the telephone. Ah, there it was by the till behind her. Mrs Lewis came out and handed her the number. Carrie had little to no experience of handling a phone, apart from answering it once or twice when she had been over at Ivy's. She tried to calm herself down before lifting the receiver. It would be no good asking her in there to do it. She was in a worse state than Carrie was, the flippertygibbet.

The doctor himself answered. Nervously, she explained the position as accurately as she could from what she had seen.

"Can you and Mrs Lewis remain there until I arrive and make sure nothing is disturbed further?"

"Yes. Yes. We can, we will."

"Good. Now I shall phone the police and we'll be there as soon as possible. Try and keep calm, the three of you." Carrie was nodding. "Mrs Thomas, are you still there?" Carrie nodded again, then it dawned on her that he couldn't hear a nod.

"Yes, yes, Doctor."

"One more thing. Is there access to the back of the premises with room for cars?"

"I don't know. Shall I go and look?"

"If you would, please." Guessing that she was not familiar with phones, he quickly added: "Just put the phone down by the side, not back in its cradle, understand?"

"Yes. I er, I'll go and look now." Carrie scuttled through to the back door, unbolted it, looked out, shut and rebolted it and scuttled back to the phone again. "Yes Doctor, there is room."

"Good woman. I'll be there as quickly as I can."

With great relief, she replaced the receiver. She could hear Godfrey still breaking his heart and felt so sorry for the poor boy. She paused a little before going back into that room. She didn't know how much more she could take of all this pain he was going through. How much longer would she have to stay here? She was desperate to get home, to see Albert. He would be worried sick by now as to where could she be. She hadn't left a note, thinking she wouldn't be out for more than an hour or so. He wouldn't believe any of this. She couldn't believe it herself. She made a move towards the door. That poor boy couldn't be left any longer at the mercy of Mrs Lewis.

Carrie straightened her shoulders and quickened her step. Godfrey was leaning forward in his chair, his elbows on his knees, his face in his hands. His shoulders were still shuddering with intermittent sobs. Mrs Lewis stood over him, an enamel mug of tea in one hand, the other patting and stroking his back. She whispered to Carrie: "He's only had a few sips," adding even quieter: "He's in a terrible state, poor love."

Of course he is, you stupid woman, thought Carrie, watching with annoyance as she put the mug down on a cupboard now and moved to crouch in front of him, putting her hands on his thighs, carefully avoiding the blood-saturated knees of his trousers where he had knelt beside his father's body.

"Have a few more sips, God. It will do you good, calm you down a bit."

He shook his head slowly, not removing his hands. Mrs Lewis, with a look of abject misery on her face, said "Aw!" and caressed his thighs gently. Carrie rolled her eyes heavenwards.

The cars arrived. Two of them, one with the doctor, the other with two policemen. Carrie heard the doors bang and went to open the back door. Dr Tilsbury was the first to enter and introduced himself adding: "You are Mrs Carrie Thomas, the woman who phoned me?"

"Yes."

The doctor took her hand in his. "You did it very well, under such dreadful circumstances. Thank you."

A police inspector and a sergeant entered behind him and nodded politely in her direction before following Dr Tilsbury across the room to where Godfrey sat. By now, the sobbing had ceased, some of the tea had been drunk and Godfrey's manner had gradually altered from hysteria to one of stunned shock. Carrie impatiently signalled to Mrs Lewis to come to her side, out of the doctor's way. With four men now in the room, God knows what she'd get up to, fluttering her eyes and butting in, when they all had a lot to see to! She obeyed reluctantly, after one final pat.

The two policemen joined the women and began to question them. Told where the tragedy had occurred, the inspector went to look briefly at the scene, then returned, took out his notebook and pencil and continued the interrogation. Between the two of them, the women related all that had happened since Godfrey had entered the Cop and they had returned with him to the butcher's.

The door was locked and Godfrey had the keys? Yes.

Was the back door locked during Godfrey's absence, did they know? Yes, Carrie had unbolted it on Dr Tilsbury's instruction to go and see if there would be room for their cars out there.

"Fine. That's fine, ladies. Thank you. You've been very helpful. That will be all for now. I just need your names and addresses. But could you both stay just a little longer here with Godfrey, while we take a look around?"

Both women nodded, Carrie reluctantly, Mrs Lewis eagerly, before making a beeline back to comfort him. Dr Tilsbury beckoned to Carrie.

"Are you alright, Mrs Thomas? You're looking quite pale. Would you sooner go home? You don't have to stay, not if you don't feel up to it."

Carrie would love nothing better than to do just that, but how could she? Someone had to keep an eye on that silly woman. If she was let loose among them they'd get nothing done.

"No, I'm fine. I'm alright, just a bit shaky, that's all."

"Well, that's perfectly understandable after this terrible shock you've had. Dreadful. Dreadful business. I'll get Mrs Lewis to make you a strong, fresh cup of tea but I want you to have a little sip or two of this first and sit, don't stand. Please."

He took a little bottle from his bag, poured a small amount into a cup and handed it to her.

"I don't know how much longer I'll be here but I'll run you home as soon as I can or find someone else to do it. Alright?"

"Yes. Thank you, Doctor."

Carrie sat in an old armchair not far from the door to the coldroom with the cup of tea in her hands, sipping it gratefully. That, and whatever the doctor had given her, were beginning to warm her up and causing the shivers to subside. Mrs Lewis sat next to Godfrey, far enough away from her to leave her in peace. She was glad of that. She just didn't have the energy to get involved in conversation with her any longer. The woman was getting on her nerves and Carrie was losing patience with her silly behaviour. Anyone would think she was enjoying all these goings-on. Why didn't she leave that poor boy alone? You could see he didn't want her fussing around him. His head was back in his hands again.

Carrie leaned back in her chair and closed her eyes, trying to switch off all these thoughts flying through her mind. Snippets of the conversation between the three men now ensconced in the coldroom wafted out to her.

"Both doors were locked. No-one could have entered the premises from outside." That was the inspector's voice, she thought, abstractedly. "And from what the women said, all Godfrey's movements seem to be accounted for. It depends on what time this death occurred, of course. Doctor?"

"I can't pinpoint it, naturally. All I can say is death occurred about an hour ago, maybe more, maybe less."

"Mm. Perhaps forensics will be able to tell us a bit more on that score."

Carrie opened her eyes. He thinks it could be Godfrey! The doctor spoke, voicing her thoughts.

"Surely you can't suspect his own son, Inspector!"

"Well, you see, Doctor…" His voice was patronising with a touch of professional jealousy in its tone, "… statistics prove that in the great majority of murders, someone close to the victim is often responsible." There were murmurs from the other two. "So you have to keep an open mind in such cases."

The doctor spoke again, with derision. "That's ridiculous! Ask anyone who knows the family. His father idolised him and you couldn't find a more devoted son!"

"That's as maybe, but you have to keep an open mind in such cases." There was a pause, then, "But to be honest, I think it is highly unlikely in this case. The knife is still in his own hand and the way the body is lying, it doesn't look as if it could have been placed there after the event. Yes, I think we can rule out murder. Now then, suicide!"

The sergeant could be heard giving a nervous chuckle. "Huh! You'd hardly take the trouble to slice through a side of pork first, if you intend to cut your own throat straight after, would you?"

The inspector's voice was now slightly threatening in his reply to his subordinate. "Alright, sergeant, we are fully aware of that, thank you. We are going through a process of elimination, aren't we? Using the correct procedures."

"Sorry, sir."

"I should think so. No, I think it's an accident, alright. A terrible, tragic accident."

He walked back into the room, followed by the other

two, his notebook and pencil still in his hands. He paused and wrote in it, wetting the pencil in his mouth now and then, putting them both in his pocket as he turned to the doctor.

"I suggest you take the lad home now, sir, and help him to break this terrible news to his mother. We'll carry on here for a while until forensics arrive."

"I'm a bit concerned about Mrs Thomas," broached the doctor. "She's got a long way to go and is in no fit state to walk there on her own after her shocking experience. She should have transport of some kind."

"Don't you worry about that, sir, I've already thought about it. My sergeant will run her home now. It shouldn't take him more than half an hour or so."

Carrie and Mrs Lewis rose to their feet as the doctor approached them. He spoke to Carrie, knowing her by now to be the wiser of the two, with Mrs Lewis looking and listening over her shoulder.

"You can both go home now. The sergeant will take you, Mrs Thomas, in the police car. Is that alright?"

Carrie didn't care if it was on a motorbike pillion, just as long as she could get home to Albert and the sooner the better.

"You know you will both be required to attend the inquest at a later date, do you? It will probably be just a formality, nothing to worry yourselves about."

They looked worried but said nothing. He walked over to Godfrey's chair and put his hand on his shoulder.

"Come on, son. Let's get you home, eh?"

Godfrey looked up at him and rose slowly, letting the statement have its full effect.

"Home. Oh, God, Mam, my Mam! What do I tell her? How do I tell her?"

His face crumpled and the sobs and tears began again. Mrs Lewis rushed in front of him and held him close, her hand on the back of his neck, forcing his head down onto her shoulder.

"Oh Godfrey! You poor, poor boy. There, there." She was crying too, now. Carrie, standing behind her, felt the tears rise in her own eyes at the thought of Mrs Parson having to hear about it all. Then suddenly, something very strange happened, wiping all other thoughts instantly from her mind. For just a moment or two, she witnessed a complete change come over Godfrey's face, as if a mask of misery had slipped to reveal one of amusement. The tight, screwed-up creases of pain and grief smoothed away and Godfrey was smiling to himself!

It had gone as quickly as it had appeared. No, she must have imagined it. She must have. How could she even think such a thing? He was a nice, tidy boy. Everyone thought so. They couldn't all be wrong, could they? She had never heard anything bad said about him. People thought highly of him. Especially Margaret Pierce. She idolised him, that was plain to see by the look on her face this morning when he asked her out. She had seen it several times before on a Friday when he had come into the shop. Oh, how she wished she hadn't been there this morning, this Friday. The thirteenth.

CHAPTER 7

Carrie Confides in Albert

THE POLICE SERGEANT put his hand gently under Carrie's elbow. "Let's get you home Mrs Thomas, away from all this."

She nodded and walked unsteadily, glad of his support, to the car.

"Would you rather sit in the back or in the front?"

His hand was on the front door handle as he asked. She inclined her head and he opened it, closed it quietly behind her, walked around to the other side, got in and started the car.

"Will there be anyone there when we get you home, or anyone I can fetch for you? You shouldn't be on your own."

"It's alright. Albert, my husband will be there. He's on afternoon shift."

"Oh, that's fine. I need to have a few words with him, explain what you've been put through."

Carrie didn't reply this time. She sat, looking out through the windscreen but seeing nothing – only that smirk on Godfrey's face.

Albert stood on the doorstep of 2 Duke Street getting more and more anxious as time went by. Where on earth had Carrie got to? It was well on the way to twelve o'clock and still no sign of her. She was never this late if she'd gone shopping on afternoons. Five more minutes. If she wasn't home by then, he'd go over to his daughter's to tell her about it, see if she knew where she was.

A black car came round the corner from Parry's Terrace. A police car by the look of it, thought Albert, distracted by its appearance. What was that doing up here? he mused, then rushed to the gate as the car pulled in and stopped by the house. Carrie, looking pale and withdrawn, was sitting in the front passenger seat. Albert had the car door open before the policeman pulled on the handbrake.

"Carrie! What's the matter love? What's happened? Where've you been? Are you alright? You're as white as a sheet!"

He helped her out, putting his arms around her as she stumbled. She turned to face him, holding on to him tightly and burst into tears.

"Oh Alb! Oh Alb!"

He looked up anxiously at the sergeant.

"Let's go inside, Mr Thomas. She needs to sit down. She's had a terrible time of it these last few hours. A terrible time. You sit with her while I make you both a strong cup of tea, then I'll tell you all about it."

Albert sat her down in her armchair by the fire, then rummaged quickly in the dresser cupboard to find the small bottle of whisky kept there for medicinal purposes. He passed it to the policeman who took it, nodding his approval saying, "I think you'll both benefit from a drop of this in your tea."

The tea made and poured, the sergeant sat with them and went over the whole story, leaving out the most gory details for Carrie's sake. She sat there saying nothing but gripping Albert's hand tightly through it all.

An hour later, he got up to leave, telling Carrie to take things easy and informing Albert that he would phone the colliery manager to tell him Mr Thomas would not be in work until Monday due to the circumstances.

No sooner had the door closed behind him, than Carrie, very agitated, tried to voice her suspicions and worry to her husband.

"He smiled, Albert! Godfrey was smiling! A sneery sort of smile. I saw him! It was only for a second or two but I definitely saw it! Mrs Lewis had his head on her shoulder. He must have thought no-one could see it. I don't think he saw me. But what if he did? He couldn't have done that, could he? Killed his own father? He wouldn't have, would he? Oh, Albert, Albert!"

She was trembling all over, her face crumpling, her eyes terrified. Albert was frightened for her.

"Calm down, Carrie love, calm down. You're not making any sense. Look, finish your tea. Try and relax a bit, please."

He poured a little more of the whisky into her cup. "Here, now sup that all up and when you've finished we'll go through it all again, in your own words, from the beginning, one step at a time."

Albert's calm approach, the whisky and the comfort and security of being in her own home gradually achieved his aim. She began to cool down and think more clearly, everything starting to slide into place and sequence. Slowly and sensibly now, she was able to relate in detail from the moment Godfrey had entered the Cop until the inspector had told the women they could leave as Godfrey was to be taken home to see and tell his mother.

"That silly woman caught round him again as he got upset again, pulling his head down onto her shoulder. I was standing right behind her, waiting for her and that's when I saw it. That's when he grinned. No mistake about it, Albert, he grinned."

She had finished all she wanted to say, all she could say.

Albert sat silent beside her for several minutes before taking her hands and squeezing them.

"Well done, love." He could picture it all now and try to work it out. He thought he had the answer, lifted his eyebrows, opened his palms and said, "Well, there you are Carrie! From what I can see, Godfrey, in the midst of all this, was probably thinking along the same lines as you were – 'that silly woman', eh? Everyone knows what she's like, she'll grab at any chance to get her hands on male flesh. She thinks she's doing them a favour. She pictures herself as a vision of beauty that every man desires!"

Albert gave a little chuckle and Carrie's lips widened a fraction as she playfully slapped his wrist and told him to 'behave'!

"Oh, she is pretty, fair play, give her her due, in a film-starry sort of way, granted, but when she opens that mouth of hers and acts up, that personality of hers leaves a lot to be desired!"

Carrie smiled a little, in agreement. Of course! Albert was right, she had let her imagination run riot, what with the shock of it all. A weight fell from her shoulders. Suddenly very serious again, Albert said: "I'm sure Godfrey could never have done such a dreadful thing, love, not in a million years, rest assured on that score. You just think about it. The knife was still in Gilbert's hand, wasn't it? And his body on top of it. Look at it logically and you'll see your suspicions are groundless. I wouldn't mention what you saw or what you thought to anyone else love. It could be dangerous."

Carrie, almost convinced now, nodded in agreement. To think she had been as near as 'damn it' is to swearing to mentioning it to the sergeant during her drive home, right on the very verge of it. She wouldn't mention it, there would be no fear of that. The doubt still lingered that Godfrey had been responsible but, she realised, that could make things very dangerous for her.

"Right," said Albert, relieved at this outcome. "How about we have a bit of dinner now? You need a bit of food inside you to settle your stomach after all the churning it's been through."

"Oh, I've got nothing in. I was going to get you some lambs' hearts before…" She got up. "I'll go and see what I can find…"

"You stay where you are, my girl. We'll have corned beef and chips and I'm making them!"

CHAPTER 8

Esther is Told

THE DOCTOR DROVE his car up to the row of semi-detached houses behind the main street with Godfrey and the inspector sitting in the back seat.

"What's the number lad?" he asked, quietly. "Fifteen, is it?"

"Yes, about halfway along. The one with the blue hydrangea by the gate." He took out his handkerchief, wiped his eyes and gave his nose a good blow.

"You alright now, son?" asked the inspector, with concern. Godfrey bowed his head and began fishing in his pocket for his keys, then sorting through them for the one to the front door and holding it visibly in his hand.

"She won't open the door if we ring. She never does. She can't handle strangers."

"There's no need to explain, son. Both the doctor and I have known your parents for years." His voice was laden with sympathy. "We'll get all this over with as quickly as we can." Although he had another reason for accompanying – and that was to observe the son's reaction on relating this bad news to his mother and if possible, banish any lingering doubt as to his involvement.

The car pulled to a stop and the three men got out, mounted the few steps to the path and walked to the front door, Godfrey preparing himself mentally for the role of concerned, protective, caring son. He was the man of the house now, after all, wasn't he? Pausing to take a few deep breaths, he lifted the key to the lock with a shaking hand, opened it and entered, calling out, "Mam, it's me! Where are you?"

"Godfrey?"

They all looked up. She had come to the top of the stairs, a bundle of dirty washing in her arms. Seeing the men at the bottom, she dropped the bundle and grabbed the banister. She attempted to say his name again but only got to the first sound before the violent jerking and thrusting took hold. Godfrey bounded up the stairs two at a time and put his arm around her shoulders, before bringing her carefully and slowly down.

"Let's go into the kitchen, Mam."

She looked up at him, her staring eyes frightened and questioning, her head still convulsing. Dr Tilsbury moved forward to help, taking her other arm as they reached the bottom step. Once she was seated in the kitchen, he opened his bag, took out a phial and syringe and gently rolled up her sleeve. Esther couldn't object, query or complain. Her whole body now was out of control. What was happening to her? Her eyes flitted from the doctor's to the needle as he carefully inserted it into her arm, saying as he did so, "This will help you Esther. Don't worry, just try and relax a little for me, if you can."

Several minutes passed and the jerking gradually subsided. Still with terror in her eyes, she looked at the three faces now focussed on hers. Godfrey, who had been standing to one side of her, now reached for a kitchen chair, moved it and sat in front of her. The two men were sitting opposite her at the table. Her son leaned forward and took both her hands in his.

"Mam," he paused for effect, swallowed, shifted about a

bit on his chair and began again. "Mam, we've got to tell you some bad news."

Esther sucked in her breath. He shifted about a bit more.

"Dad's had an accident in the shop. A very bad accident. I'm afraid he's..."

The colour drained from her face, she fell back in the armchair, the jerking returned and a scream struggled in her throat to escape past her clenched teeth. Both the doctor and her son rose to their feet as Esther rose to hers. Godfrey held out his arms to her, sobbing as she fainted and fell into them. The two men rushed to his side. The inspector was sure now, having witnessed his reaction, that Godfrey was totally innocent. Murder, he concluded, was out of the question.

By the time Esther had regained consciousness, the sedative was fully effective.

"He's dead, isn't he, God?"

He moved his head slightly forward.

Tears ran silently down her face. Bed would be the best place for her now, suggested the doctor, and followed behind as Godfrey insisted on carrying her up the stairs.

"I'll go and fill her hot water bottle," he said when he'd laid her in the bed and pulled up the blankets. "She's as cold as ice."

"How is your mother up there, now?" asked the inspector as, bottle in hand, Godfrey reached for the kettle, checked if it was full and lit the gas.

He didn't answer, just shook his head, as if afraid to speak.

"Here, let me do that for you," said the policeman getting up. "You go and sit for five minutes." He took out a packet of Players and offered it to him. Godfrey gratefully accepted. All this was taking it out of him. He was dying for a smoke.

"I'll pop up with the bottle. I have to ask your mother one or two questions before I go."

Entering the bedroom, he handed the bottle to the doctor, whispering as it was put in place, "Is it alright if I have a few words with her? Is she up to it, do you think?"

Dr Tilsbury nodded. "But you'll have to make it quick. She's on the verge of sleep, now."

He approached the bed. "Um, Mrs Parson, I'm so sorry but I have to ask you. Was Gilbert in any sort of trouble, with the business or anything?"

She shook her head slowly and mumbled, "No, the business is fine."

"Was he worried or depressed about anything that you know of?"

She shook her head again, more vigorously this time. "Today was our wonderful son's twenty-first birthday. He was full of plans. How could he be?"

"I understand, Mrs Parson. That's fine. That's all I have to know. I'm leaving now. You have a good sleep and look after yourself."

Both men walked onto the landing, closing the door quietly behind them and stood there at the top of the stairs talking.

"Well, that's that cleared up," said the inspector. "I'd better get back now, check what forensics have come up with, if anything."

He'd been right then, by the looks of things: murder out, suicide out, leaving only accidental death. He walked down the stairs ahead of the doctor and into the kitchen, saying as he went that it was the obvious conclusion, really, going by the position the body was found in. Knowing from his own conclusions now that the boy was innocent, he looked at him in a different light and went up to him, putting his arm round his shoulder.

"Your mother is sleeping peacefully, up there."

Poor beggar, he thought, for this to happen on his twenty-first birthday. All he had heard about the boy, from his own father, the doctor, Mrs Lewis and Mrs Thomas and many others over the years must be true. They couldn't all be wrong, could they? A thoroughly good son, through and through. A rare thing these days, right enough. Some might even say he was too good to be true!

"Give me the shop keys, Godfrey. I'll see to everything down there, lock up when we've finished and return them to you as soon as I can."

Godfrey sorted them and handed them over.

"Thanks."

"Here's a number for you to ring, should you want to get in touch with me about anything." He put out his hand with the words: "You take care now, son, of yourself and your mother."

"Oh, I'll look after her alright, don't you worry!"

The doctor, meanwhile, was delving into his bag again and brought out some tablets. He handed them to Godfrey.

"These are mild sedatives. Both your mother and you can take them. They might help a bit over the days to come. The dosage is written on the box – and don't exceed it. If they're not suitable, I can change them for you. Now, you've got my number, if there is anything else I can do, please don't hesitate to ask."

"Thanks Doctor, for everything."

"How are you feeling now? Able to cope with everything, do you think? Is there anyone I can contact to stay with you? Keep you company? Help you through this terrible time? You shouldn't be alone."

"No, really. I can manage. I can't have my mother upset anymore than she already is. I know her. I know what she's like. She won't want anyone else." His voice was firm. The doctor's, in reply, was sympathetic.

"Alright, son, alright. I'll tell you what I'll do. I'll arrange for the district nurse to call later and twice daily over the next few weeks, or until after the funeral, whenever that will be, just to help out a little and keep an eye on your Mam, if that's alright with you. Nurse Bevan. Rowena. I think your mother knows her, doesn't she?"

Godfrey agreed. He could manage that, two visits of twenty minutes or so, most of which would be spent having a cup of tea, no doubt, and dodging questions. She was a right old gossip but he could handle her. It would suit him and keep the doctor off his back.

"And what about the business? The customers? You'll need to give that some thought. I can see to that for you, mind, if you'd let me. I know quite a few of your father's friends socially. I could ring round, see if there's a butcher's assistant somewhere who could keep things ticking over for a few weeks. Shall I arrange it?"

Godfrey looked very relieved. "Oh, if you could. That would be a great help. I hadn't thought about any of that!"

"Well, naturally. It would be the last thing on anyone's mind, in the circumstances."

"Dad would want that, to keep things going. The shop is… was… was his pride and joy." The mistake in the tense was deliberate and had the desired effect.

"I'll go ahead with it then and make some arrangements. Don't worry about it and I'll keep you informed. I'll phone later to check on your Mam and let you know what is happening."

"Oh thanks, Doctor, you've been a great help. Dad's got some true friends." This time he didn't change tense, noticing the tears welling in the doctor's eyes.

"Right. I'll be off then. Phone me, mind Godfrey, any time of the day or night if you need to. I'm only a street away."

"I will. And thanks again for everything."

He shut the front door after him and went straight up the stairs into his parents' bedroom. He stood looking down at his mother, now fast asleep.

"One down, one to go, eh Mam?" he whispered, grinning with satisfaction.

Esther's head stirred on the pillow.

CHAPTER 9

Wilfred Breaks The News

THE COP WAS filling up. Margaret was glad of that – less time for the others to tease her about her 'date' but they took every opportunity, nevertheless.

"Who's the lucky one then, eh? Hooking the pick of the bunch!"

"What are you going to wear tonight, Maggs?"

"Bet you'll be sitting in the 'courting' seats at the back!" The last two rows of seats in both cinemas consisted of doubles – two seats with no centre arm – and they were very popular.

"Behave, you lot, will you!" but she was smiling at them, not cross. She still couldn't believe what had happened earlier on. Her wildest dreams had come true. Godfrey had asked her out – her secret love no secret anymore! She was walking on air and couldn't wait to write to her best friend, Pauline Edwards, Carrie's granddaughter and the only one who knew of her infatuation. After tonight, she'd have such a lot to write to her about!

As she served one customer after another, her mind pictured the evening ahead. She would wear the new jumper she had just finished knitting, a two-ply white one with short sleeves and a lace-like pattern, with the grey, circular skirt that Vera Roberts had made for her. Oh, and her wide black belt to match her flat black shoes. When dinner-time came, she would slip up the street to Woolworths to buy a new bright-red lipstick. Oh, and a small bottle of Lily-of-the-Valley perfume.

The teasing continued all the morning, Moira joining in whenever Maggs had occasion to enter her 'office', which was quite often, as crates of fresh fruit and vegetables, large tins of biscuits, cartons of tea and several other things were stored in there.

"I can see you walking down the aisle now, before I've even found a bloke!"

"Don't you start! I've enough to put up with from that lot in there. Even Mr Williams has had a go at me!"

"Nice though, Maggs, isn't it? You and Godfrey. That's a match made in heaven, if ever there was one!"

"Oh, go on with you! We haven't had one date yet!"

She returned to the shop, her arms full of fresh cabbages to replenish the vegetable rack. As soon as she entered, she was brought to a halt by a tangible change of atmosphere in the whole room. People suddenly stopped talking and turned round to look at her. Alarmed, she slid her eyes over the crowd. They came to rest on Mrs Lewis-the-Post who was standing close to Mr Williams. What did she want back here? What was she whispering to him about? It was obvious that it was something about her, and not something complimentary by her shiftiness.

Mrs Lewis had been told by the sergeant, as she left the butcher's: "I would appreciate it if you kept all this business to yourself for a while. It will all get about soon enough."

She had nodded and agreed, putting her hand reassuringly on his forearm. "Of course, I understand."

Well, she had kept it to herself. For over an hour. She couldn't any longer. Besides, she had discovered she'd run out of potatoes!

Margaret suddenly felt uncomfortable and vulnerable. She straightened her back. Her conscience was clear, there was no gossip to be spread about her. But she had to find out exactly what it was that woman was saying, and now! Dumping the cabbages in a heap in the stand by the window, she turned and marched over to them both, caught the woman's arm and spun her round to face her.

Angrily, she said, "If you've got anything to say about me, Mrs Lewis, then have the decency to say it to my face!"

There was a communal gasp from the rest of the customers as Mrs Lewis shrank backwards. Mr Williams put out his arm to restrain Margaret. She shook it off and stood her ground.

"Maggs, wait! It's not what you think. It's bad news, I'm afraid." His manner and voice were very quiet and sympathetic. "Let's go into the back room, eh?"

He led her towards the door, passing Joan and Sarah, who stood back to let her pass. They were staring at her too, with tears in their eyes. Her hand flew to her mouth. She blurted out to them both: "Mam! It's my Mam, isn't it! She's been taken bad!"

Both of them moved towards her, shaking their heads, their arms out and crying openly now. Wilfred stepped in again, motioned them to step back, guided her through the door and closed it behind them. She made a grab for her coat and bag, he stood with his back against the door and held up his hands.

"No, Maggs, it's not your Mam, love. Sit down, there's a good girl." She dropped onto a chair, he pulled another one up and sat before her.

"It's got nothing to do with any of your family but it is bad news, I'm afraid."

Her mind was running riot. What could it be?

"It's about Godfrey Parson. His father, Gilbert, has had

a nasty accident, a fatal accident, in his shop this morning, while Godfrey was over here."

Her mouth fell open and her hands clutched her throat as she gasped for breath. Wilfred related the gist of what he had heard, then got up, saying quietly: "Moira's going to walk home with you now, love. Go the back way, up the canal bank. It will be quicker for you and you'll meet less people."

She shook her head. "No. No, I want to stay. I'll be alright." Her face was wet with her tears.

"No, Maggs. Listen, love. Terrible news like this will sweep through the village like wildfire. Everyone will know about it. And the fact that he asked you out this morning. Each one will want to offer you their sympathy. You'd be in tears all day, in front of them. Far better to be home for that, eh?"

"But it's Friday, Mr Williams. How can you manage short staffed?"

"That's for me to worry about, love. Now, home you go."

She desperately wanted to see Godfrey, hold him in her arms, comfort him. But she knew she couldn't. She had no right. Just a casual assignment for a first date didn't give her that right. What he must be going through! And his poor mother. How on earth would she cope with it? Now, in the midst of all this unbearable sadness and grief, that poor woman would be thrust into the company of endless strangers. Godfrey would have to bear all that worry and stress she'd be going through, on top of his own grief. Her heart went out to him. He had been so happy, light-hearted and carefree this morning. His twenty-first birthday and then to cross the road, enter his shop and discover... She closed her eyes tight. It didn't bear thinking about.

CHAPTER 10

The Days Go By

TIME, INEVITABLY, WENT on, hour by hour, day by day, not quickly enough for Godfrey and agonisingly slowly for Margaret Pierce, who saw or heard nothing of him or from him. The inquest came and went, giving a verdict of accidental death, as was expected by all, except Carrie Thomas. The gut feeling she had experienced on seeing that smirk on Godfrey's face refused to go away despite Albert's reassurance and explanation and she wanted so much to believe it. She had gone over it and over it in her mind ever since, reliving the moment and trying to work out what had really happened.

The funeral came and went with Esther, flanked by Dr Tilsbury and her loving and attentive son, suffering her tremendous ordeal with courage and determination. Life dragged on for all involved: Godfrey, planning for his future; Margaret, pining for her lost love; Esther, persevering bravely for the sake of her son; and Carrie, helpless but unconvinced.

At the Parson household a routine had quickly developed after Gilbert's death, with Godfrey staying at home with his mother and the district nurse calling twice daily to check on her. Once the funeral had passed, things were altered. Esther patently hated those visits and Rowena's condescending attitude – treating her like a child with her "How are we today, then?" and "Shall we get up and dressed this morning?" That 'we' made her so angry, which stimulated her stammering, making it worse, doing nothing to calm her or help her. She just wanted to be left alone, she complained to Godfrey.

"Just you and me. We only need each other, we can handle things together, by ourselves, can't we?"

And so, within a few days, Rowena's visits were brought to an end.

"I think it's for the best, Rowena," Godfrey explained. "She gets so worked up every time that door bell rings. It's not helping her. She's best left alone. She's used to it. It's what she prefers."

"But I thought she was getting used to me, to my visits."

There's none so blind as cannot see, as the saying goes, he thought. Esther, he knew, would have made her feelings quite clear.

"She gets up and about as soon as you've gone."

"Really?!" Disbelief was in her voice.

"Oh yes. She is improving gradually. And I'll look after her. I only want what's best for her. You know that."

"Of course you do. We all know that. But what will happen when you start back to work? She'll be hours in the house on her own. Someone should be popping in to check on her. Grief can do some very funny things to people, you know, especially if they've got time to brood over things."

There was no-one else to do any 'popping in' as yet, but Godfrey had plans that he was sure would work out. First though, he had to get shot of this gossipy busybody.

He said, casually, "Oh, that's all taken care of, my girlfriend will be doing that. It's all sorted. I've already spoken to Mam about it. She knows her and she likes her." He cleared his throat before adding, with a catch in his voice, "So did my Dad. She's very happy about the arrangement."

"She never mentioned it to me!" Rowena was hurt by this exclusion of confidentiality.

"You know Mam – she can be a very private person. Don't take it personally." Keeping his eyes on Rowena's face as he talked, he added, "She's always on at me to settle down, you know what mothers are like. It's my first girlfriend, though, and I've only just started seeing her, so I hope she won't jump to any conclusions!" He liked to hedge his bets. Her professional frown of concern cleared a little. Godfrey smiled to himself, as he added, "Just the thought of what might develop is helping her get through this."

Rowena relaxed and smiled back at him now. He could see plainly what she was thinking: that this was something for the poor woman to look forward to then, her son courting at last, maybe even getting married in the near future and grandchildren perhaps, in a year or two! He was obviously wanting to do what was best for his mother, fair play. Mm. Perhaps it was for the best then, to let them to it – to sort things out on their own. She would have a word with Dr Tilsbury and explain things and advise him that, in her opinion, now would be the best time to terminate her visits to the Parson household, that she herself would be perfectly happy with the situation. He always valued her point of view! She gathered her things together.

"And who is this lucky girl then, Godfrey? Do I know her? Is she local?"

I knew you'd ask that, you nosey bitch, he thought.

"Margaret Pierce. She works in the Cop."

"Oh yes, I know her. Oh, she's a lovely girl, Godfrey. You've made a good choice there!"

He walked with her to the front door.

"Thanks for all you've done for us, Rowena. I don't know

how we would have managed without you over these last few weeks."

Always the thoughtful, kind lad, was Godfrey! She shook his hand.

"I'm just glad I could be of some assistance to you both. Say goodbye to your mother for me, won't you, and give her my best wishes."

Phew! She was gone at last. Now he had to move quickly before the nosey nurse had time to stick her oar into his plans. He hadn't intended Margaret's name to come out just yet. Still, no harm done. He sensed she could be manipulated any-which-way he wanted. He ran upstairs to his mother's bedroom. First things first.

Sitting on the edge of her bed, he asked, "Mam? You awake?" She turned round to him asking anxiously, "Has she gone?"

"Aye, she's gone, Mam and for good. She won't be back."

Her head fell back onto the pillow with relief.

"Oh, thank goodness for that! Thanks, God."

He paused for a little while, fidgeting a little then spoke hesitantly.

"Uh, Mam, I've got to go out now, down to the Cop to see about our weekly order. I don't want to phone it in this week. There's something I have to do, someone I have to see."

Concerned by his tone of voice, she sat up.

"What do you have to do? Who do you have to see? Why? Will you be long?"

He settled himself a little further in on the bed, took her hand and asked, tentatively: "Mam, do you know Margaret Pierce? She works in the Cop."

Esther nodded, picturing her face and remembering the Wednesday afternoons she and Gilbert had spent in their shop while Godfrey was away on National Service. Gilbert would take her down to do the accounts and help with the orders and cleaning. She had enjoyed those days, working together, chatting, seeing people passing, waving to them through the window, but safely cocooned from involvement. Gilbert had pointed Margaret Pierce out to her.

"See that young lady there, Est? Now, there's a lovely girl. She would be perfect for our Godfrey. I've told him that! He'll never find a better one. She's been in our shop lots of times and she likes him too, I can tell. I've seen the way she looks at him."

Esther had moved to the shop door to peep through the Venetian blinds and get a closer look without being seen.

Gilbert had joined her and whispered, "I always let him serve her, if I can!" They had chuckled over that bit of conspiracy. "I think he likes her, so there's hope, eh?" Esther had liked what she was seeing and hearing. "He's so slow off the bloody mark though, Est. I haven't heard him call her by name yet! Someone else will snap her up if he doesn't get a move on! Old Wilf speaks very highly of her, says all the customers love her."

They had both watched as she had swept the front of the Cop, stopping to chat and smile as people passed. Gilbert had said wistfully, "She'd be perfect for him. Perfect." And Esther had nodded in agreement. "I feel like giving our son a bloody good kick up the backside!" Esther had nodded again, laughing.

Godfrey had been demobbed now for over six months and she hadn't heard her name mentioned once by him and Gilbert and she had almost given up hope. All this had flashed through her mind before Godfrey spoke again. She held her breath. Hesitatingly, he began.

"Well," he fidgeted again, "I asked her out on the day that Dad had his…" He paused, his eyes filling up on cue. "… I haven't been able to see her since. I haven't had the chance or the courage."

Esther reached out a hand, impulsively.

"Will you be alright on your own for a bit, Mam? While I pop down and…"

She grasped his wrist and shook it, encouragingly.

"Of course I will! You go, son. I'll be fine."

It was the reaction he had fully expected. He knew from the hints his father had continually dropped that it was what both parents wanted.

"Uh, Mam…"

"What, son?"

"Would it be alright if I asked her to call? Here, to the house? Would you mind?"

Esther was beginning to get very excited. She would not let her affliction get in the way of this. She was determined. She would cope. Giving his wrist another little shake, she whispered: "I would love to meet her, God!"

He let out his breath in an expression of relief.

"Ask her today. Go on. Ask her to tea today."

Again it was the response he expected. He got up and kissed her forehead.

"Thanks, Mam! You'll love her, I know you will."

He moved to the wardrobe, opened the door and took out a half-bottle of whisky hidden there behind some shoes. He poured a good measure into a glass on the bedside table and handed it to her. She took it gratefully but with a guilty look.

"You knew about it?" she said, meaning the hidden bottle. "It's just that I wake in the night sometimes. It helps me to sleep."

Why should he mind? He had encouraged it from the day his father had gone. It was part of his plan.

"Mam, what harm can a drink do, now and again? On the contrary, it's been a big help to you, hasn't it? Don't worry. It doesn't bother me, honestly!"

She sipped the liquor, licking her lips between the sips.

"I think you need one now to calm you down a bit, eh? I don't want you getting all het up about this visit."

She waved her hand, dismissively. "I'm actually looking forward to it, God."

"You are? Oh Mam, that's great! I'll be off then. See you later."

She emptied the glass. It did help, a lot, and had done ever since that terrible day. It blurred everything in an unreal sort of way, relaxing her, distancing her from her troubles, making her feel lighter somehow, everything seeming less terrifying. She had come to rely on it now and Godfrey didn't seem to mind. He had just said so, hadn't he? In fact, he often brought home a bottle or two, so that she wouldn't be without. He didn't know about the stock behind the couch in the front room, by the look of it, or he wouldn't be buying it. Gilbert had brought a boxful home from the wholesalers just before he... They both used to enjoy a small glass every night before they retired. She hadn't told him about the box. She wouldn't bother. It was comforting to know she had some in reserve, just in case he forgot to get some.

But Godfrey did know. He had sung the praises of a tot or two and had encouraged her, knowing full well that she would come to depend on it. Every evening, after 'that

Rowena woman' as his mother called her, had gone for the day, he and she would sit by the fire together talking and, as Godfrey was quick to tell her (and frequently remind her), never once during those evenings with a little whisky inside her had she found any difficulty with her speech – a fact that had already registered in her brain. It had become her prop.

She would get up in a minute or two and have a nice bath and shampoo, do some baking ready for this evening and get out her best tea-service and give it a wash. Our Godfrey courting! Oh, if only Gilbert was here! She poured herself another little tot.

Chapter 11

All Goes Well

It was just after 9 a.m. when Godfrey entered the Cop. Margaret had her back towards him as she stacked packets of Indian Prince tea into a fixture. Wilf saw him enter and slipped swiftly into the staff-room leaving her in the shop on her own. Joan and Sarah were in there, opening a wooden crate of tightly compacted dried fruit to tip into a tin bath and crumble up ready for weighing into 1lb-sized blue paper sugar bags. He motioned to them both not to enter the shop.

Margaret, hearing someone cough, turned and said automatically, "Yes?" and gripped the counter as she saw who it was.

"Hello, Maggs."

"Godfrey! How are you? How is your Mam?"

"Oh, I'm fine. We're both fine, thanks. Well, sort of." Silence for a few moments while they stood looking at each other, then they both spoke at once.

"I've been wanting to come down to see you, but couldn't."

"We've all been so worried for you both." Then: "That's understandable," from Margaret again and, "We're fine, really. Coping slowly," from Godfrey. Silence again and shy smiles from the both of them.

"I, er, I've brought our book in. There's a lot to go down from the counter-book – a couple of orders, I think and, um..." his voice caught in his throat, "two ounces of pipe tobacco." He cleared his throat, fully aware of the effect it was having on Margaret. "Oh, and I've brought in this week's order for today's delivery if possible."

"I'll do it now. Straight away." She took his book, opened the counter-book and started entering the lists of items.

While she had her head down, he spoke again, softly. "Maggs, I'd like to ask you out again, but my mother can't be left alone for too long, just yet." Her pencil stopped writing but she didn't look up. "So I was wondering if you could, if you would, like to call up to the house sometime?"

She straightened up. "Would your mother mind?"

He brushed her question aside. "Gosh, no! She would love it if you did! In fact, she told me to ask you." Sheepishly now, he continued: "I'd been talking to her about you."

Margaret's heart was thumping.

"Oh. Tell her yes, I would love to come, Godfrey. Thanks."

Wilf, listening, had come into the shop. Godfrey still had more to say.

"Today? After work, perhaps?"

Margaret was flustered now. "Er, I can't. I'd have to let my mother know first. She'd worry where I was."

Wilf, now carrying on with the fixture filling, turned round and butted in. "That's no problem, Maggs! Write a note explaining things and give it to Frank. He's taking deliveries up your street, later."

Godfrey jumped at this suggestion, smiling broadly. "Right then! It's number fifteen, Maggs." He laughed a little, nervously. "But you know that, of course – you write it on our order boxes." She smiled, nodding. "See you about quarter to six, then?"

"Oh, but it's Friday! We don't finish till half past six on Fridays."

Wilf winked at him. "She'll be there boy, quarter to six will be fine."

"Thanks, Mr Williams."

With Godfrey's order completed, Margaret wrote a note for her mother telling her she would be home later than usual, the reason for it, and could she put the following items in a bag and send them back with Frank. During her afternoon teabreak she had a quick wash and change in the staff-room while Moira helped out behind the counter with the big orders in between her desk work.

"Thanks, Moir. I'll make it up to you whenever I have a chance."

"Course you will. What are friends for, anyway?"

*

Esther Parson stood back to look at the table, very pleased with the result. The tea was laid out on a beautifully embroidered white cloth. Three places were set ready with her delicate, violet-patterned bone china. There was a plate of lean, sliced, boiled ham, another plate filled with small sausages individually wrapped in crispy bacon, a freshly-baked quiche, still warm from the oven, a dish of small tomatoes, picked from the greenhouse in the back garden, a trifle and a rich, dark yeast cake, sliced and buttered. All were neatly arranged around the table centre.

It was just gone half past five. Godfrey was upstairs getting ready. Just time for a little drink before their guest arrived. Esther went into the kitchen, took a recently opened bottle from a cupboard and poured herself a small whisky. She put it to her lips just as her son appeared.

"You deserve that, Mam," he said approvingly. "That table in there looks fantastic! Thanks."

She raised her glass to him. "I'm glad you're pleased with it, son. Here's to our special guest. I hope she enjoys her visit."

"Oh, she will, I know she will." With a look of concern, he added: "Are you sure you feel alright about this now, Mam? Do you feel up to it? I don't want you to be under any pressure. It's not that long, after all, since… I don't want you getting upset or anything."

"I'm fine, son. Really. Honestly. I'm quite looking forward to it. I can see you are happier and that makes me feel happier. Your happiness is what means the most to me, matters most to me: your happiness, your future. You are young, you have the whole of your life in front of you. To see you settled will make what is left of mine a lot more bearable and contented."

He was crossing the room towards her, his arms out ready to embrace her, when the bell went.

"Ah, there she is!"

"Well, go on then, quick!"

He turned and left to answer the door. Esther drained her glass and took a few deep breaths.

Godfrey, opening the front door, put out his hand. "Margaret! Thanks for coming." She stepped in and he helped her off with her coat. "You look nice."

"Thank you."

As they walked down the passage, he halted and whispered: "Er, Maggs, if you smell whisky on my mother's breath, please take no notice. It's just that she's very nervous and she finds it helps her with her speech, you know – the stammer – when she meets people."

She nodded, eager to put him at his ease. "It's OK. I understand. Don't worry, Godfrey."

He ushered her into the rarely-used dining room where a fire now burned brightly and welcoming in the tiled grate. Esther was there, waiting. Godfrey introduced them, deliberately acting up on the formality.

"Mam, this is Margaret Pierce, whom I believe I've mentioned once or twice! Maggs, my mother, Mrs Esther Parson!"

He finished with a slight bow, as the women chuckled and shook hands, saying simultaneously: "Nice to meet you!" It broke the ice.

The meal passed very pleasantly, all three joining in easy conversation. Margaret complimented Esther on her cooking, Esther offered to give her the recipes, Margaret related news and bits of harmless chit-chat she'd heard in the Cop and Esther remarked, prompted by Godfrey, on the visits of Rowena, the district nurse. Mostly, he sat back, leaving them to it and feeling very pleased with himself. There was only one small hitch, as far as Esther was concerned, when her convulsions threatened. They had finished the meal but still sat chatting at the table, discussing films. Esther was about to say that *Gone with the Wind* was her favourite. Gilbert had taken her into town to see it when it had first come out. But that very first word, combined with the happy memory of that wonderful evening surfacing in her mind and the calming effect of the whisky now wearing off, prevented that first letter coming out from behind her clamped jaw.

Margaret, reading the difficulty she was in, instantly and intuitively distracted her. "I hope you don't mind me butting in, Mrs Parson, but did you knit that jumper you are wearing? I've been looking at the pattern all evening and have been dying to ask. I haven't seen one like that before."

It worked. Esther looked down at it pulling it out with her thumb and finger to see the pattern herself. "What, this? It was in the *Woman's Weekly* a few weeks ago. It's a very easy pattern to follow. Do you like to knit, then?"

Margaret nodded, pulling out her own jumper as evidence.

"Oh, that's pretty, isn't it God? I've still got the magazine if you want it. I keep them all," said Esther, completely recovered now. "I'll look some out for you to browse through."

She got up from the table.

"Let's go and sit in the parlour. God's lit a nice little fire in there for us."

Godfrey butted in. "You go on in, Mam, and sort out those magazines ready and Maggs and I will clear away. Put your feet up for a bit." He wagged his finger at her. "You've had a very busy day today."

He knew, full well, she would agree and make a beeline for yet another hidden bottle. She was really getting hooked now, needing it little but often. So far, with her daily intake, she had managed to appear and sound normal but he'd have to watch her closely from now on.

"You don't mind, do you Maggs, giving me a hand in the kitchen?"

"Don't be silly!" she answered, gathering up some of the dishes. "After a beautiful meal like that, washing up is no chore. I would have offered anyway."

Once in the kitchen, Godfrey whispered "I wanted to have a quiet word with you, about Mam and our situation and things."

She busied herself at the sink while he talked.

"The thing is, Maggs, I'd like to ask you out on a proper date but I can't leave Mam on her own for long yet. I was hoping to start back full time in our shop next week but it would mean leaving her on her own the whole day. Rowena, the district nurse, was calling around dinner-time but Mam made me stop her calls. She doesn't like the woman, can't seem to take to her, as you heard her say earlier. She would get wound up every time the bell went. That wasn't doing her any good as you can imagine. If I can find someone suitable to pop in, say halfway through the day, it would mean I could work straight through and spend most of the evening with her and have an hour or two off now and again, to see you. But there's no-one I can think of. Do you know of anyone? A customer or a neighbour of yours who could…?"

He deliberately left the question in the air and it had the desired effect – Maggs paused and looked up at him.

"I could do it, God! I could pop up in the dinner hour. It's only a few minutes walk."

He put his hands up, shaking his head. "No. No way, Maggs! I can't let you do that. Sacrifice your dinner-hour? It's hard work behind that counter."

"Nonsense! Of course I could. It would just mean eating my sandwiches here instead of in the staff-room. I'd love it and I think we get on great, don't we – your Mam and me?"

Godfrey appeared to be weakening. "Oh, she likes you, alright. I know she does. She hasn't stopped talking about you since first thing this morning! I can see she's very much at ease with you, already." He jerked his head in the direction of the dining-room. "I noticed what you did in there, too, about that jumper of hers."

"Well, there you are, then. Let me do it. Please."

"Well," he hesitated, "only on one condition, then. She

will want to cook a proper meal for you. She'll insist on that, I know she will. You would have to agree to that!"

"After that delicious meal tonight, I'd be a fool to refuse, wouldn't I? Anyway, that will give her something to do and occupy most of the morning for her, won't it? And she'd have to join me. It would be my turn to insist! And that will make sure she has a main meal herself. See? It's all beneficial to her well-being. It's the perfect solution!"

Godfrey put down the tea-towel, put his hands on her waist and kissed her lightly on the nose. She was so easy to manipulate, like putty in his hands!

"Maggs, you're brilliant!" He took her hand and pulled her towards the passage, suitably excited in his manner. "Shall we go and tell her?"

CHAPTER 12

Now Is The Time

THE WEATHER WAS cold with a biting east wind. Christmas had passed and Godfrey was bringing the accounts up to date. The shop had done well again, very well indeed, better even than his father had done the year before. Part sympathy profit, thought Godfrey, grinning to himself. He knew he was popular with the customers and that they all felt sorry for him. They popped in more often these days and bought a variety of other items apart from their weekly rations. He'd had to restock on packets of dried herbs, suet, sauces, condiments – all sorts of things. It wouldn't surprise him if the Cop sales were down! Of course, he realised the real reason for this increase in his popularity was Margaret Pierce. They'd begin by enquiring after his mother's health, sending her their best wishes, ask how he was and if he was coping alright and gradually get round to mentioning Margaret, singing her praises, voicing their approval. Some even jokingly asked when was he going to set a date, make an honest woman out of her!

Never, if he could help it, he thought and there was no likelihood of a shotgun wedding either! Margaret Pierce was a 'good' girl – everything below the waist being strictly out of bounds. Not that that bothered him. There was plenty of that to be had if you knew where to look and he knew where to look alright, keeping it far enough away from his own doorstep. It took just a phone call to meet up with the boys again, now and then, for a night on the town, to ensure he didn't miss out on anything. As to how he was managing things, he was doing very well, thank you! Everything was doing fine and his plans were heading steadily in the right direction. It wouldn't be long now, he just had to pick his moment. He leaned back in the chair, very pleased with himself. Everything was working out just as he had intended. Maggs and his mother continued to get on well with their daily dinner-breaks and most Saturday afternoons or early evenings, he managed a short date with her, taking her to the cinema or into town – a bit of a bind – but necessary to keep her sweet. They had often asked Esther to join them but she always refused insisting that they spent some time alone.

"You don't want me playing 'gooseberry'. You're young, go on, both of you, enjoy yourselves, shoo!"

Besides, Godfrey had installed a television set for her and he kept replenishing her whisky supply. He thought of everything to keep her content, bless him. Most of Sunday afternoons, he and Margaret spent at the butcher's, she doing all the tedious cleaning and Godfrey sorting the meat for the week ahead. Yes, everything was going along hunky-dory, week following boring, monotonous week, especially those long treks all the way up to Stephen's Street taking his 'girlfriend' home! Still, not for much longer, now.

The next thing on his agenda necessary to his requirements was a car. He had already picked one out: a nice little blue Austin Seven. That would suit the situation for now. This time next year he would swop it for an MG hopefully. He put his books away and made a phone call. The car he had ordered would be delivered to his house this afternoon. Monday, today. Right, then. This Saturday night would be the night. Just a few more days. The adrenaline started pumping through his veins at the thought of it.

Later, at half past five, just as the Cop was closing, a blue car pulled up outside the shop and out stepped a man. Joan, Sarah, Maggs, Moira and Wilf gathered by the shop window and looked out curiously as Godfrey closed the car door behind him, walked to the shop and entered.

"Evening, everybody! Anyone want a lift anywhere?"

Joan and Sarah squealed in unison. "Yes, please!"

Godfrey laughed. "Come on then, but only to the bus-stop, mind! How about you, Maggs? Want a lift home?"

"In this weather?" she asked, grinning from ear to ear. "What do you think?"

"Moira, Mr Williams?"

"You've got a car full already, son," said Wilf. "No, we're OK thanks. We haven't quite finished up here yet. There's all the locking up to do. You lot carry on."

The girls all piled into the car, Maggs in the front, the other two in the back, oo-ing and ah-ing as they examined the interior. They reached the bus-stop in less than five minutes, dropped the two passengers off and continued on up to Stephen's Street.

"What do you think then, Maggs? Like it?"

"Do I! I love it, it's lovely. And so comfortable. What a surprise! You never said."

"Better than walking all the way, eh? After a hard day's work. Should save on your shoe leather from now on."

"First a television set, now a car. What next, Godfrey?"

"Ah!" He tapped his nose. "Who's being nosey, then? Maybe another little surprise of some sort."

"Another one?"

"Wait and see. I've got plans!" He certainly did have plans. Margaret's imagination took flight. What could it be? Not an engagement ring, surely? It was far too soon. They had only been going out together for about seven months. She would say yes, though – no hesitation. Wouldn't she? Oh, what if it was?

Godfrey was thinking along different lines, picturing how the weekend would turn out, mentally rehearsing how it would proceed. "Mm, she's in for more of a shock than a surprise!" he thought casually.

"What does your Mam think about it? The car? Does she know yet?"

"Of course she does. I had to ask her first, didn't I? I can't just go and spend her money!" Not yet, anyway but give him time, he thought. "She was all for it. She was the one who insisted I should run you home tonight. And every night, from now on. She's given me orders!"

Maggs slid her arm through his and squeezed up closer to him.

"I'm so lucky, God!"

"How's that, then?"

"To have you and your mother in my life. Two of the nicest, kindest people I've ever known."

*

Saturday arrived. Margaret, as she always did on Saturdays now, walked up to Esther's when the Cop closed for the day at one o'clock. Esther would have the dinner nearly ready and they would all have the meal together. Then Godfrey would do some of the rounds in the van with Margaret helping, until they reached her street and he would drop her off. Normally, he carried on and finished the rounds about 7 p.m. when he would return home, see his mother settled and ready for bed, leave and walk down to the Cop to meet Maggs, who would be on her way down from Stephen's Street. The next few hours he'd spend with her, either taking her to a local cinema, a local dance or one of the milk bars that were cropping up everywhere. Afterwards, he'd walk her home, taking the quieter, more secluded (and shorter!) route up from lower Crymceynon along the canal bank, stopping now and again, for the expected 'romantic' kiss and cuddle. Maggs loved Saturdays and looked forward to them every week. Little did she know that the night didn't end there for Godfrey. A quick phone call to Dudley Bowen and they would both be off in his mate's car, coming home in the early hours, his mother, too, oblivious of his absence.

This Saturday followed the same routine up to the point where he dropped her off from the van. He had cut the round short and she was home by half past four. Instead of meeting her by the Cop, he said, he would pick her up at her house, in the car.

"Be ready before seven, Maggs. We are going to Cardiff!"

Cardiff! She spent a lot of time getting ready for this treat, puzzling over what to wear, trying out different shades of lipstick, choosing jewellery from her small collection and dithering over whether to wear high heels or flat shoes. At last she was ready. Elsie-May studied the result from her armchair, pride in her daughter shining from her eyes.

"You look a picture, Margaret. You wouldn't look out of place on the arm of a prince!"

Her daughter laughed out. "I think you're a tiny bit prejudiced there, our Mam!"

Her mother motioned with her hand, her finger pointing to the floor, her wrist circling. "Turn round, let me see."

Margaret obeyed, posing with her hand on her hip. She had dressed to suit the weather, in a skirt of warm, woollen material, patterned in a small check of white, black and beige. It fitted snugly over her flat tummy and rounded hips, opening out into box pleats that flared as she moved. She had knitted herself a twinset, matching the wool to the beige and wore a 'pearl' necklace and earrings she had bought in the market 'over-the-other-side', to set it off. Seamed nylons and black court shoes accentuated her shapely legs. Her mother clapped her hands together in total approval.

Maggs was putting the final touch to her lips with a clear red lipstick and giving her shoulder-length dark, wavy hair a final brush when the doorbell rang. She grabbed her black handbag, slipped into her warm, grey, winter coat, kissed her mother and ran.

"What time will you be home?" shouted Elsie-May after her.

"I don't know, Mam," she shouted back, "but don't worry and don't wait up. I've got my key safe. Bye!"

Godfrey hadn't spent the last couple of hours worrying about his attire and appearance. He had other things to see to. Home before five, he let himself in with his key and found his mother sitting in the middle-room, watching television and sipping a whisky, one of several she had had by the look of things.

"Alright, Mam?"

"Oh, Godfrey! You're home early. That's nice."

"Yes. I told you I was taking Maggs to Cardiff tonight, remember? So I've left the debt collecting till Wednesday." He moved to the fire, bending over it to warm his hands. "Brr! It's damned cold out there!"

"It's damned cold in here!" she said wryly. "My feet are freezing with the draught under the doors."

"Mm, best place for you is bed on a night like this, tucked

in with a nice warm bottle and one of your Agatha Christie books. Have you had your bath?"

She shivered. "No, it's too cold for that, too!"

"I don't blame you." He walked towards her. "Your hair could do with a wash though, Mam."

She put her hand up to it. "Could it?" She forgot things a bit these days. She couldn't remember when she had last washed it. Days seemed to run into each other lately.

"It's not like you, Mam, to neglect your hair. Shall I give you a hand to wash it? Then you can get straight into a warm bed and have a good wash in the morning."

She touched her hair again, dithering. "Have you got time, God? I don't want to hold you up."

"I'll make time for you, Mam, you know that!"

"I would like it done, love, now that you've mentioned it. Maggs will be calling tomorrow, won't she?"

"Right then, Mam. Let's get a move on, eh? I would like to be from here just after six if I can but I want you settled in bed before I leave. Then I can relax and enjoy the evening, knowing you are safe and warm." Esther got up, a little unsteadily. What Godfrey wanted always came first with her. "You go on up and change into your nightie and dressing gown, then and I can put a towel round your shoulders, so you don't get wet. I'll get your hot water bottle filled while I'm waiting."

Within ten minutes she was ready and Godfrey had placed the bottle in the bed, denting the pillows and crumpling the sheet so that the bed appeared as if already slept in. He now filled a jug with warm water from the bath tap and when his mother bent over the wash-basin, tipped its contents over her hair. Applying the shampoo he gently massaged it in. "Right, that's done. A quick rinse now Mam and we're finished!" He filled the jug from the bath tap again. This time with cold water. "Ready?" Over it all went in one go, taking Esther's breath away.

"Oh, Godfrey!" she gasped. "Oh! That was stone cold!" She lifted her head up, her wet hair hanging over her face and dripping onto her nightie.

"No! Oh, sorry, Mam, I'm so sorry! Are you alright? I must have used the wrong tap in the rush!" He lifted the towel from around her shoulders onto her head and began to rub it vigorously. "Damn! Your nightie's all wet in the front. I'll get you a clean one." He helped her out of her dressing gown. "This is dry, thank goodness. Put it back on when you've changed and leave it on in bed until you've warmed through."

He rushed to her bedroom and returned with the clean nightie, a glass and a bottle. "Here, have a tot of this before you undress. I don't want you catching your death of cold!" Liar, he thought! "I'll wait outside while you change. Shout when you're decent."

Esther swallowed the whisky, gratefully, put the glass down beside the bottle on the cupboard, changed her nightie and shouted. "Ready, God but where's my dressing gown? I can't find it."

"It must be there somewhere." He entered the bathroom and had a quick look around. "Well, that's a mystery! Did you take it into your bedroom?"

"No, I don't think so."

He picked up the bottle and glass again and handed them to her. "Look, take these and get into bed. It's too cold to hang around. I'll find it and bring it in."

"Oh God, you're going to be late. It's all my fault."

"Nonsense! Mam, get into bed, will you!"

Shivering, unsteady, worried and confused with all this rushing about, she made her way out onto the landing. Godfrey, the dressing gown now in his hands, having been quickly retrieved from where he had hidden it, watched until she neared her bedroom door, right opposite the top of the stairs, then he rushed out, calling her.

"Here it is, Mam. Found it!"

She stopped and turned, awkwardly as he bumped into her deliberately. She fell backwards down the first three steps that formed a bend at the top of the staircase, hitting her head on the passage wall and dropping the glass and bottle. They rolled and bounced down the stairs, smashing into smithereens on impact with the tiled floor below. Esther landed on her back on the widest part of the third step down, her shoulders against the passage wall, one leg bent awkwardly beneath her, the other stretched out in front of her on the narrowest part of the step. Half stunned, she tried to rise but her free foot had no place to grip. It slid off onto the step below. She lost her balance and with her arms out, grabbing at thin air, she fell down the rest of the flight to land heavily, in a heap on the broken glass. It was all over in seconds.

Godfrey clutched the banister, watching and waiting. There was no sound, no movement. He took off his shoes and socks, switched off the bedroom and bathroom lights and crept carefully down the stairs, keeping to the side by the banister and carrying his footwear. At the bottom, he grasped the newel post firmly as he swung his body round to the passage, away from the scene of the 'accident'. He skirted along the wall to the porch door, deposited his shoes and socks there and turned off the two-way switch, sending the hall and landing into sudden darkness. He waited a few seconds for his eyes to adjust to the light coming from the kitchen, then made his way carefully along the wall again until he reached there. Hurriedly, he finished dressing, scooped up his wallet, keys and a small torch, turned it on and the kitchen light off then retraced his steps to the porch door again, pausing to listen for the slightest sound. There was none. He opened the door wide and left it open, feeling the strong draught blowing in from under the front door while he put on his shoes and socks. He would carry no trace of glass or smell of whisky into his car. He moved the front door mat in a little to allow more draught through, then quickly left the house, shutting the front door securely behind him. Confident and in high spirits, he got into the car and drove off.

Chapter 13

Another Accident

The whole evening had been chock-full of excitement for Margaret. She hadn't been to Cardiff much, and never at this time of the day with all the lights shining and crowds of people all dressed up with somewhere to go. Godfrey had parked the car in a quiet side street near the city centre and they had walked a short distance to the New Theatre. He was taking her to a proper theatre, to see a proper, professional play, not an amateur one like the annual week of plays that circulated the villages and were held in the Workmen's Hall in Crymceynon! And she had always loved and looked forward to seeing those. What a treat! Just wait till she told the girls in the Cop. And Pauline, in her next letter!

The wind was blowing a gale when they came out again and they ran, laughing, back to the car.

"Are you hungry?" Godfrey asked her. Suddenly she was.

"Mm. Ravenous!"

"We'll stop somewhere on the way home, then. I know of one or two places that are still open, this time of the night."

They soon found one and sat in the car, their newspaper parcels on their laps. They opened them and tucked in as if they hadn't eaten for days. Food had never tasted so good. Warmed through now, inside and outside, Margaret stretched herself, luxuriously, with her arms over her head and kicked off her shoes.

"Oh, I enjoyed those. I've enjoyed the whole, wonderful night!"

"Good," said Godfrey. "So have I!"

"What time is it?" she asked, sleepily. Godfrey held his wrist to the car window to catch some light from the shop.

"Um, twenty past twelve." The time had flown. "Ready for the 'off' again?"

"Mm." She lay back comfortably in her seat. "Home, James!"

"Right, my lady! We'll stop at my house first, OK? Just to check how Mam is and let her know we're home safe."

Maggs nodded.

"We could stop a bit and have a nice milky cocoa, if you like. Finish the evening off."

Margaret didn't want it to finish. "Mm, yes, I would like."

Godfrey leaned over and whispered in her ear. "Then we can take our time saying 'goodnight' outside yours!"

She giggled, almost purring, as she moved her head to rest against his shoulder. The car started up again and Maggs was asleep within minutes.

"Maggs! We're home."

She stirred beside him. "Mm? What, already?" She fished for her shoes.

"I'll run up to put the light on and get the milk on to warm. Take your time, sleepyhead, there's no hurry."

He needed to enter the house alone – the opened porch door would be hard to explain. Besides, he wasn't sure what he would find. His mother was a tough old bird. She might have survived. He doubted that though. What the fall hadn't accomplished, hypothermia would have, surely: draught, thin clothing, wet hair, stone tiles – he was confident of the outcome.

Margaret, still drowsy, took her time. It must be nearly half past one now. Another hour or so wouldn't make much difference; everyone at home would be fast asleep and she had her key. She had never been out this late before, not even on VE night.

She found it hard to believe how much people's lives had changed since then, and hers in particular. Changes to her home, her family circumstances, to be in a job she thoroughly enjoyed, the new friends she had made there, time and money to spend on herself without feeling guilty – and Godfrey – the man she loved and had done from the beginning! Her next letter to Pauline would contain all these thoughts and more. Margaret had missed her company so much in those years after she had passed to enter grammar school but they had since picked up from where they left off, spending hours together whenever Pauline came home from university. They could tell each other anything and everything – always had done – things they wouldn't even tell their own mothers, knowing instinctively they could both trust each other with their confidences.

Godfrey walked up the path slowly, listening for the car door to shut and then the gate. He needed to time this right. There was a squeak as the gate swung to and a click of the latch. He slid his key into the front door and opened it, took a few steps into the porch and reached for the two-way switch, his hand hovering over it just as Margaret stepped in behind him. He flicked it on and the hall lit up. Godfrey froze, his hand still on the switch. Margaret's eyes focussed immediately on Esther lying on the tiles before them and her hand flew to her mouth.

"Oh, my God! Oh, my God!"

Her teeth started chattering as she, too, froze to the spot. Godfrey stayed motionless for a few seconds longer then moved forward, whispering: "Mam? Mam?"

His voice and movement drew her attention to him. She put her hand on his arm and restrained him gently. She could see the woman was dead, literally stone-cold dead. Her bare legs, arms and face were a horrible shade of blue.

"Don't God, don't touch her. It's no good love, she can't hear you."

He knelt beside the body, touching his mother's face, smoothing back the still damp, tangled mass of hair around it. His body started shaking with convulsive sobs.

"No. Not again. Oh, Mam, no!"

Margaret leaned over him, taking his hands in hers.

"Godfrey, come away love. Please. You mustn't."

He looked up at her face, then with her help, rose to his feet.

"What do I do, Maggs? I can't think. Help me. What do I do?" He gripped her tightly.

"Sh, God, sh."

"Not again, I can't go through all this again! I don't know what to do."

Tears were streaming down his face now. She patted his shoulders, taking control of the situation.

"There's nothing you can do, God. We need to phone someone – the doctor, the police... Come and sit down." He looked up at her, alarmed.

"Don't worry. I'll see to it. You just sit there."

Thank goodness they had decided to call at the house together, she thought. He could never have coped with all this on his own.

"Dr Tilsbury! Oh hell, what's his bloody number?" He got up in a rush and walked back into the hall, where the phone sat on a small table. He opened the drawer and began fumbling furiously through a little book of telephone numbers, turning the pages quickly and muttering to himself: "Tilsbury. T, T, under T," all fingers and thumbs in his haste. Margaret took it from him.

"I'll do it. Sit down, God."

With a grateful look in his eyes, he said pitifully: "I'm so glad you are here, Maggs," and sat obediently on the chair by the telephone, watching as she found the number and dialled.

The doctor arrived within twenty minutes and Margaret let him in.

"The police are on their way," he said, moving towards the body. "This is a pretty kettle of fish again, isn't it, for that poor boy? Where is he?"

"In the kitchen."

He stood looking down at Esther. It was obvious she had been dead for some time. He looked around at the broken glass and caught the still strong smell of whisky as he drew in his breath. The bell rang. The police had arrived, the same two that had dealt with Mr Parson's 'accident'.

"Bloody hell," said the sergeant, impulsively, taking in the whole scenario at a glance. He lowered his voice so only the inspector could hear. "To lose one parent by an accidental death is bad enough. To lose two seems bloody careless, in my opinion!"

"Enough, sergeant!" said his superior sternly and with a look to shrivel him. "No-one's asking for your opinion."

An hour later, the five of them all sat in the cold kitchen. The fire was out and they all still had their coats on. The questioning began: What time did they come home?

Maggs and Godfrey stared at each other, puzzling and trying to remember. Margaret answered. "About half past one, quarter to two, was it, God?" Godfrey shrugged his shoulders slightly. "Yes, about then, I think," said Maggs.

Where had they been and what time had they left the house to get there? This time Godfrey answered. "After half past six, getting on for seven, I think." He glanced at Maggs for confirmation.

"Yes, he arrived at my house about ten minutes to."

"And how was your mother when you left her?"

"She was tucked up in bed, with her book. I'd put a bottle in for her. She had wanted to wash her hair, ready for tomorrow – today," he corrected himself. "Maggs comes to dinner on Sundays. She wanted to look her best, as always." He gulped and his face crumpled. He took a deep breath and continued. "I persuaded her not to, or thought I had. It was too cold. Her hair is thick. It takes a long time to dry." Another gulp. Margaret took his hand in hers. "She must have changed her mind, after I had gone. She can be strong willed on times. I shouldn't have gone. I shouldn't have left her." He went the whole hog now and broke down. Silence from the others until he had gathered his composure again.

"Er, about the broken whisky bottle and glass, son. Did your mother like a drink?"

Godfrey looked up at the policeman, offended by this question. "How do you mean 'like a drink'?"

"No offence, son, but I have to ask. As you must be aware, a broken bottle and glass were found where she lay."

"She wasn't an alcoholic, if that's what you're implying," he said angrily. "My parents would enjoy just one small drink each before retiring every evening. Dad would buy a boxful at Christmas and it would last them the whole year and more. The last box is still behind the couch in the parlour, untouched, as far as I know."

The inspector nodded slightly to the sergeant, who quietly left the room.

"Mam still had one small one, before going to bed. It helped her to sleep, she said and it gave her a little comfort since Dad…"

The inspector turned his attention to Margaret.

"Did you ever see her taking a drink?"

"No, but I knew she would have a small sip or two, before I called." She looked at Godfrey, almost apologetically, as she added: "Godfrey said she found it helped her to control her stammer a bit whenever she had to endure meeting people, since Mr Parson…" She squeezed Godfrey's hand again looking at him sympathetically, then added: "But I never saw her drink."

The sergeant returned and whispered in the inspector's ear, who wet his pencil and wrote in his notebook. He cleared his throat.

"Uh, Godfrey, that box in the parlour. It's empty!"

"Empty?"

"Empty."

"It can't be! There were six full bottles in there. The box was sealed. I carried it in there the Christmas before last. There were two left in the last box that I took out. I gave them to Dad and burned the box." That would account for his fingerprints, should they find any. "I even bought her a bottle or two, so I could keep her company of an evening. I didn't like the taste of the other one. She said she preferred it, too." He paused, staring into space, smiling a little and nodding his head. "It did seem to help her through everything at the time. Helped her to relax and cope with everything she had to deal with."

"Did she ever appear to either of you as being the worse for drink? A bit tiddly, perhaps?"

They both shook their heads, then Godfrey focussed, suddenly.

"Twelve bottles!" he said, disbelievingly, "in eight months! Surely we would have been bound to spot it!"

The doctor intervened. "Not necessarily. She probably drank the most at bedtime and sipped it through the day. And twelve bottles – you'll probably find there's still quite a lot of that left lying about, hidden, in strategic places."

Again, the sergeant was sent off with a nod to hunt them down. He found six with varying amounts still in them, one each in the kitchen, the dining room, the parlour, the bathroom and two in her bedroom.

The questioning finally finished by around five o'clock, the conclusion, reached by the police, being that Mrs Parson had got up and washed her hair soon after Godfrey had left, taking the bottle and the glass in with her, so she could warm herself up with a tot as she towelled her hair. Then with the bottle and empty glass in one hand, she had switched off the bathroom light and made her way back to her bedroom in the dark – as there was no light left on in there, according to Godfrey and Margaret, when they arrived back. Maybe she had heard a noise or something, downstairs or was simply disorientated in the dark and cold and turned right instead of left.

"Her bedroom door being situated where it is, right opposite the top of the stairs," said the inspector to the sergeant.

The sergeant nodded in agreement, thinking to himself, "He's not such a bad b★★★★★d really and he's damn good at his job, I'll give him that!"

CHAPTER 14

A Change of Mind

ANOTHER INQUEST WAS held and another verdict of accidental death recorded. Another funeral was organised with half of the village turning out to pay their respects. And another huge wave of sympathy washed over 'poor Godfrey'! What that poor boy had suffered through these last nine months or so! But at least this time he had that sweet girl, Margaret Pierce, to help, comfort and support him. '*Na ferch hyfryd*. The best thing for those two now, would be to get married as soon as things settled down a bit, was the general opinion.

Godfrey, on his return to work soon became fully aware of what the majority was thinking. Snippets of overheard conversation with surreptitious glances in his direction, hints as big as bricks from some of the more outspoken, and polite enquiries as to "How is Margaret?" from others, made it clear to him that to dump her now or in the near future wouldn't do him any good. He wouldn't want that, everyone turning against him – finding out he wasn't the man they thought he was! He began to think of the plus side of marriage to her. She was easily fooled, manipulated, gullible. He could still have his freedom when he wanted it, take time off to have some fun, make up excuses. She'd swallow it. Mm. He could have the best of both worlds. She wasn't a bad looker when all was said and done. He had noticed the envious glances from other blokes when they had been out dancing and, as a matter of fact, he had felt quite proud with her on his arm as they walked up the canal bank of a Sunday evening, passing all the other courting couples. Another big plus in her favour was her energy. She kept the house – his house now – in perfect order in her 'spare time', ironed his shirts the way he liked them, helped in the shop whenever he wanted her to. She was content just to be in his company, he didn't even have to spend much of his lovely money on her, taking her places, buying her presents. She could keep her job on at the Cop for a few years too. She was used to spending a night out with the girls there, now and again – he would be sure to encourage that. On a Friday or a Saturday. Those nights would suit him best. Yes, all things considered, marriage to Miss Margaret Pierce could be the best move to make. His mind was made up.

In June, four months after his mother's funeral and just a year since he had first asked her out, he proposed to her and she immediately accepted, throwing her arms around his neck and hugging him. With his head over her shoulder he allowed himself a quick, satisfied grin before his next move. He slid his hands to her waist and leaned back a little to look her in the eyes. His own eyes welling with tears now, on cue to heighten her sympathy, he looked downwards and hesitatingly began: "Maggs, I, er… you'd want – I know, like all girls do – but I can't, I couldn't…"

He left that hang in the air until she'd respond, as he knew she would.

"Can't what God? What's wrong?"

"You'll want a church wedding, with all your family and friends there and all that goes with it." He paused for effect, then carried on in a rush. "And I'd have no-one. I can't face that. I'd break down, make a fool of myself, ruin everything, I know I would…"

Church was totally out of the question as far as he was concerned. The only God he worshipped was himself. And the three weeks reading of church banns, giving anyone a chance to come forward about anything untoward that he'd been up to on his nights out – he didn't trust his own friends that much! And that brother of hers, Brian, or her father, might be tempted to ask around. Get it all over, as quick and as quiet as possible, that's what he wanted.

Maggs hastened to reassure him. "God, I just want us to get married, I don't need a church wedding and all that fuss. It's you I want. Nothing else matters, it's not important, honestly."

You're a smart one, Godfrey told himself – *she's so easy to handle!* He put his hand in his pocket and took out the small box containing his mother's engagement ring, removing it and slipping it on her finger. Surprisingly, it fitted. No expense there then and very little to be spent on the wedding now, too. It would be a Register Office affair with just Maggs, her parents, Pauline, Dudley and himself, the reception afterwards to be held at 'his' house.

The wedding was fast approaching – just three more weeks to go. Now that Godfrey had achieved his aim of getting his hands on the money at last, he was beginning to feel very frustrated about his future. It hadn't all turned out quite the way he had expected. His feet were itching to get out there and spend it, but he couldn't. He started to doubt his decision about this wedding. He should have just sold up and gone. His patience was wearing thin. But on the other hand it was far too soon to show his true colours – people might, would, turn against him, become a bit suspicious even. No, better to wait, keep up with the façade, play the part, stick it for a year or so. Leave the memories of the double tragedy to fade, with him and Margaret blending into the background a little. Marriages could go wrong. After a while people could accept that. Blame would be cast on both sides. Then he could make his move!

Give it a year, then. He sighed deeply. A whole year before he could get his hands on an MG!

Margaret was having doubts too, the nearer it got. She sensed the change in Godfrey – a withdrawal, somehow. One minute she could dismiss the thought, explaining it away with all that had happened: losing both his parents like that was bound to have a profound effect on him; the next minute she wondered what his true feelings for her were. She kept these doubts to herself, not even voicing them to Pauline. Keeping up a front was so difficult. Her mother noticed her lack of enthusiasm, so did the Cop staff and the customers. Everyone put it down to nerves and the strain of the recent past.

Pauline sensed it too, from her letters. They were shorter and less frequent as time passed. Their style wasn't the same. Usually, Margaret wrote as she talked, her pen running away with her, like her tongue did. Something was wrong. She read and re-read every letter several times, searching for clues but found none. There wasn't enough information in them to analyse. Her instinct told her to reply, asking straight out what was wrong, what was worrying her but she couldn't. How could she interfere? It might make things worse. Margaret had to sort it herself: it was her life. Pauline would do nothing to damage their friendship. If she could see her and chat, something might emerge but she couldn't do that either. By now, there was just a week left to go and during that time it would be impossible to visit her. She had promised the two girls she shared her flat with that she would go on holiday with them. All the arrangements had been made months ago.

It had all been booked and paid for. They were going to the Isle of Wight, not returning until the Friday. She wouldn't be arriving in Crymceynon until late that night. She wouldn't see Margaret until the following morning – her wedding day.

Chapter 15

Too Late Now

THE DAY DAWNED – a lovely day, warm and sunny. Pauline slipped across the road to Elsie-May's, opened the door and shouted: "Is she up yet?"

"She's upstairs love," came her mother's voice from the kitchen, "You go on up." Margaret was still in her bed but lying there wide awake.

"Come on lazybones! I thought you'd be up and dressed by now!" She slipped off her shoes and jumped onto the bed beside her, snatching a pillow to prop against the headboard to lean against. "What's up girl? It's your wedding day! Where's your joie-de-vivre?" Margaret eased herself up into the same position, her spirits rising on seeing her friend.

"Where's my what?" she giggled.

"You're not having second thoughts are you, Marg?" there was a slight undertone of seriousness to her voice that Margaret picked up on. "Any doubts, hm?" To her surprise, Margaret nodded. Pauline's voice was full of concern now. She took her friend's hand in hers. "Tell me, then."

"Oh, I'm so glad you are here Pol, so glad you could come!" She sounded near to tears.

"What is it? Come on, out with it!"

"Am I doing the right thing, Pol? I've got this uneasy feeling in my stomach the whole time, it won't go away. It's Godfrey. He seems so different, lately. I haven't really got to know him that well, have I? Should I wait a bit longer? What do you think?" She was searching her friend's face as she spoke. Pauline didn't know what to think, what to say. She'd keep things light till more came out.

"I think 'wedding nerves', that's what I think." She paused, then added: "Ask yourself one question, Marg, and answer it truthfully. Do you love him?"

With no hesitation, she nodded. "Yes! Oh, yes!" A tear escaped as she closed her eyes and rolled down her cheek.

"Well, there you are then!"

"But I don't know if he loves me – in the same way. He's never actually said so." She looked down, hesitated, then looked up and spoke quickly before changing her mind. "There have been times, when I've been with him, when I feel as though he's not with me at all. Do you understand what I mean?"

"He's a man, Marg, a different species! They don't think like we do."

That didn't satisfy her. "What is your honest opinion of him Pol?"

"Well, I don't really know him, do I? How can I pass judgement? The last time I saw him was in Crymceynon Juniors and he was in the class above us." Margaret's eyes were pleading for help. "But from what I remember, he seemed pretty popular with everyone. Everyone seemed to like him." Margaret still wasn't satisfied. Pauline moved her position on the bed to kneel in front of her. "You've been going out with him now for how long? Fourteen, fifteen months?"

"It's a lot less than that really though, Pol. Weeks passed after both accidents when I didn't see him. I spent more time in his mother's company – before she died – than I did in his."

"Exactly! An awful lot has happened to you both during those dreadful times. Couldn't that explain this feeling you have of his absence when he's with you?" Margaret sighed and shrugged her shoulders but still looked worried. She shook her head.

"I can't explain it, Pol, I just have this continuous, sick feeling in the pit of my stomach. And that old saying – 'Marry in haste, repent at leisure' – keeps ringing in my head."

Pauline had known something was wrong but hadn't bargained for all this. She was beginning to get very concerned now for her friend. She was afraid to influence her one way or the other. If Margaret did go ahead and marry him today and it all turned out wrong, Pauline would blame herself; and if she called it off and ended up pining for him for the rest of her life, again she would blame herself.

"Oh, that's just an old wives' tale, superstitious nonsense." She'd have to watch what she said but at the same time get her to think hard about either decision. "Listen, Marg. Reason it all out for yourself. Take your time. Only you can come to any conclusion. It's a big step to take – marriage. Find out what you really want – to marry Godfrey or call it off. When you've thought it all through, I'll be downstairs waiting and whatever you decide, I'll be there to support you. But do have a good think now. Yes?" She got off the bed, put her shoes on again and bent to kiss her friend's forehead before leaving the room. She told Elsie-May her daughter was going to enjoy a bit of a lie-in.

Nearly an hour later Margaret came bouncing down the stairs in her pyjamas and burst into the kitchen, full of smiles. "Come on Pol, don't just sit there! There's lots to do. I'm getting married this afternoon!" Like young girls again, they both ran back up the stairs, nattering nineteen to the dozen.

At two o'clock the small wedding party of six was assembled at the Register Office – Godfrey and his best man

Dudley Bowen, Tom and Elsie-May Pierce, Margaret and her bridesmaid Pauline Edwards. The ceremony took place without a hitch. There followed a buffet reception back at the Parson household that went on until early evening, when the four guests left. There was no honeymoon planned. Godfrey had been on his best, most charming behaviour the whole time. The atmosphere had been pleasant and relaxed.

Pauline, walking home with Margaret's parents felt far more at ease than she had done. Elsie and Tom seemed quite taken with Godfrey and she herself had to admit to liking him.

CHAPTER 16

Married Life

LOOKING BACK, MARGARET knew deep down from that very first evening that she had made the biggest mistake of her life. She had made her bed and now she had to lie in it. She didn't, wouldn't, admit it to herself at the time. She explained away his behaviour to her then and in the months that followed, unwilling to accept she could have been so wrong.

No sooner had the door closed behind their small number of guests, than he walked back to the front room, flopped into a chair by the fireside and said: "Thank God that's over! Make us a cup of tea, Maggs, there's a good girl and bring in a plate of any food those gannets have left. I'm really hungry now!"

She had fully expected to be taken into his arms, kissed tenderly and told how lovely she looked, how he had waited all day for this moment when they would be alone together. Close to tears, she left to do his bidding. Waiting for the kettle to boil, she struggled to eliminate negative thoughts and think positively. He was tired. It was the strain. He must have missed his own parents' attendance at this big step in his life. Things would alter as time went on. They would get used to each other, have fun in their marriage like her own parents did – teasing and touching each other, snatching kisses, laughing easily and not afraid of showing affection. Soon too, God willing, there would be a family of their own to look after, to share and enjoy, to watch and to wonder at, to love. It would get better.

She filled a tray and took it in, placing it on the coffee table and sitting herself on the settee, expecting him to join her there. He didn't. The television was on – a quiz show.

She poured and passed him his tea and a plate of sandwiches, saying tentatively trying to make conversation: "I hope there will be enough wedding cake left to thank all our customers for their lovely presents. Haven't we been lucky, God? There's enough linen and china in the dining-room to open a shop!"

Without taking his eyes off the TV he took the tea and plate answering: "Now that's a good idea Maggs! I could sell 'em wholesale to my mates!" He was actually serious, she realised. "Who needs twenty pairs of embroidered pillow slips for a start!"

She had been overcome by people's generosity and fully intended thanking each one personally with a tiny piece of their wedding cake wrapped in a serviette and a small note of thanks.

"Shall we go and start wrapping up some cake now, God? I know it's our wedding day but I don't want it to dry out. Once they are wrapped I can put them in biscuit tins ready for Monday: one for your shop and one for the Cop."

"Mm? Oh, not now," he said with his mouth full, "the comedians are on next. You make a start if you want to, though – only bring a nice big slice in for me before it all goes!"

The rest of the evening she spent alone in the kitchen, wrapping little parcels of the cake, placing them carefully in the tins and writing a list for all the small notes of thanks. She would spend tomorrow evening, probably, doing those for her customers and his. It was common courtesy to show appreciation to people for their thoughtfulness and kindness. You couldn't just sit back and take everything for granted.

When the TV had closed down for the night Godfrey opened the kitchen door. "I'm off up, Maggs. I don't know about you but I'm ready for bed."

She rose and put the lids securely on the tins. "We'll do the notes between us tomorrow, is it?"

"Not tomorrow. I've got to go down the shop – get things ready for Monday."

He knew what she would say next.

"Tomorrow evening, then?"

He would nip this in the bud right now. "Hey, now hold on, Maggs! Do people normally change their whole routine when they get married?" He grinned at her. He would begin as he meant to go on. "You know Sunday nights are my nights out with the boys. I always see them on Sundays, you always see yours on Saturdays, don't you! There's no need to change that, is there? We'll be together all the rest of the week, after all!"

He turned and left the room. She switched off the light and followed him up the stairs, he to the bathroom, she to the big bedroom in the front of the house – Godfrey's bedroom – where they would be sleeping. His parents always slept in the second biggest bedroom at the back of the house, opposite the top of the stairs. Nothing but the best for their Godfrey, even where bedrooms were concerned.

Margaret opened her suitcase and took out one of the new nightdresses she had made with Vera's help. The material was white, silky and fine, the design Grecian, elegant and simple. The top of the bodice and waistline were gathered in with rows of shirring elastic, the inch-and-a-half wide shoulder straps carefully embroidered with small wild flowers in different delicate shades. The hemline reached just to her ankles, accentuating her slim shape. She picked out the one stitched with the blue forget-me-nots and rummaged in her case for her toiletry bag and hair brush.

"It's all yours!" said Godfrey, returning from the bathroom and dressed in his pyjamas. "Don't be long – I'm shattered!"

Ten minutes later she had washed, cleaned her teeth and changed into her nightdress. She brushed her hair, took a deep breath and approached the bedroom door. It was in darkness. She couldn't switch the landing light off until she could see her way. She felt around for the bedroom switch – it must be somewhere near the door. She failed to find it. She would have to ask Godfrey. Surely he wasn't asleep yet? He wasn't. He was watching as she fumbled about searching. The landing light behind her shone through the fine material of her nightie, making it transparent, revealing and outlining her figure. Pure and untouched. He was interested and sat up further in the bed. This would be a first for him!

"Godfrey," she whispered, "can you put the bedside lamp on, please. I can't see where I'm going otherwise."

The light clicked on and she walked to the end of the landing to click off that light. When she returned, Godfrey threw back the bedclothes on her side of the bed and patted the mattress. He was smiling, welcoming, inviting her in. He wanted her. He must love her! Everything was going to be alright. She relaxed a little, walked to the bed and climbed in, her eyes on him the whole time.

Click! The room was in darkness again. He took something from his pyjama pocket and groped about under the bedclothes. She knew what he was doing. Sylvia had told her, not long after they had got engaged, not to be in a hurry to start a family – "Use protection till you get used to each other, Maggs. Make life easier for yourself. Have a bit of fun first!"

Some of the older married women customers advised her that to get pregnant too soon could complicate things – "Husbands want your full attention in the beginning. They don't want you getting out of bed every couple of hours to feed and change a crying baby. Take our tip," they said, "Men can be jealous of other demands on your attention, mind!"

There were always volumes of advice to be had from the Cop customers, on any subject! She had laughed with them all but they did have a point there, she supposed.

Their love-making was soon over. Margaret, her emotions high and expectant, was left bereft. Godfrey, needful and purely physical, was completely satisfied. He soon slept. Margaret lay awake long into the night. And so a pattern was established in their marriage – she already knew exactly what to expect from it and her husband. He was selfish and would do whatever he wanted, whenever he wanted. Her needs just didn't seem to count.

For the next six months it was Margaret now who put on an act for the benefit of others, laughing over the teasing she received from customers and the staff when on her own and automatically collaborating with Godfrey's performance when they were in any company together. No-one was any the wiser, not even her own parents, as to the misery she was suffering. Yet still she lived in hope, still she tried when they were alone, submitting to his every need and still she tried to convince herself that things would improve between them, that he would realise just how much she loved him.

Week followed week, most of their daytime taken up by their respective jobs, his evenings filled with deliveries or hours in a pub with that horrible, lecherous Dudley Bowen;

hers with the housework, cooking, laundry and mending. She actually looked forward now to her Saturday nights out with the girls, to have a laugh, relax in their company and to revel in the fact that they, at least, enjoyed hers too. Sunday nights, when he was out – gradually leaving earlier and coming home later – she would spend at her parents' house or on occasion when Pauline was in Crymceynon, in her company. Now that her friend had begun teaching, their get-togethers were much less frequent. She taught at a grammar school on the outskirts of Cardiff and most of her weekends and term-ends were taken up with marking or lesson preparation. Margaret was rather relieved at this. It was much harder to keep up a pretence with Pauline. Just how much longer she could keep things from her she didn't know. She knew she would be bound to confide in her eventually. But what could Pauline do? She couldn't do anything, only worry about her and that wouldn't be fair on her friend. Divorce was impossible – there was such a stigma attached to it, especially after such a short time. Margaret wouldn't be able to explain to people, defend herself, tell people how one-sided her marriage was. It was she who would carry the blame, after what 'poor Godfrey' had gone through. That was the trouble with close-knit communities – everyone a judge or juror. And she would have to stay to face it all. She had no money to uproot herself and move away – and no chance to save any either. It was her wages that were spent on their day-to-day needs. Godfrey gave her none. He paid the main bills – gas, electricity, rates, coal and of course the car which she never got to ride in these days. There were no handouts for treats of any kind for her.

Unknown to Margaret, Pauline was getting more and more suspicious the longer this marriage went on. Her friend's letters now said far more about the girls from the Cop than they did about her husband. In fact, he was hardly mentioned. And whenever Pauline did get to see her it was always at the Pierce's house or 26 Stephen's Street – never an invite to the Parson household. That was odd, too. Margaret had enjoyed showing her all around it on the day of their wedding. Pauline was desperate to get her on her own, for a whole day at least. She would love to invite her to stay for a weekend in Cardiff but that was out of the question – she still shared a flat with two other friends and wouldn't be able to get somewhere of her own for quite a while yet. Another year, maybe, and she would have saved enough to put a deposit down on a place of her own. She would get to the bottom of things then. Perhaps things would have improved by then – you never knew! All marriages had to go through a 'learning' stage, get used to each other's ways, after all. She might be worrying about nothing. But she doubted it.

Weeks turned into months, with Margaret finding each successive day harder to bear. Even their 'love' making, still protected, was becoming less frequent but her yearning for a baby was growing ever stronger. She longed to hold one in her arms, give it all the love she had inside her and see it returned. Her mother was always dropping hints about a new grandchild these days, and customers were becoming curious as to when the patter of tiny feet would be heard in their house. Boy or girl, a combination of those two parents would make a beautiful baby, they said. She dreaded their hints and enquiries, struggling not to break down and cry in front of them all.

She never refused Godfrey's advances, hoping against hope that his supply would run out at a crucial moment or that one would break or that he would come round to her way of thinking. If only, she wished, he would change his mind and his ways towards her. She still refused to accept it was futile to crave for this to happen. She resolved to broach the subject of starting a family the next time he wanted her, to force some kind of answer from him. The way things were going, she might not have many more chances.

CHAPTER 17

Turning Point

1955. THE FIRST Saturday in January. They had been husband and wife now for almost a year and a half. It was a bitterly cold night and they had just got into bed. The packet sitting on the bedside table did not go unnoticed by Margaret. Had they been placed there casually or deliberately? The bed was warm and cosy. She had put two hot water bottles in there earlier on. This cold weather she liked to cuddle one for comfort as she hopefully drifted off to sleep. Godfrey was already in there reading the newspaper. She lay on her side, her back towards him and leafed through her weekly *Woman's Own*. When he had finished reading she sensed him reach out to the table then put something in his pocket before switching off his light. Hers remained on. As he began to fidget beneath the bedclothes she caught his arm.

"No, God, don't. Please!"

"What do you mean 'don't'? You're my wife! I'm entitled!" His tone was angry.

She spoke softly, hoping to placate him. "I mean don't use that, please! Let's start a family, God. We've been married eighteen months now. My body clock is ticking like mad, I feel like a broody hen. Please, God? I really want us to have a baby!"

Keep it light and cheerful, she thought, try and appeal to his better nature – if he had one. It seemed to work – he chuckled!

"Ticking clock? Broody hen? What the bloody hell are

you on about, woman? Start a family? Kids? You must be joking! We've got years yet for that. If ever! I'm only twenty-three! Who the hell wants to be saddled with kids at that age? I haven't started living myself yet!"

I'm still waiting for it to start, he told himself.

She tried a little cajoling. "Come on, God, it will be lovely, you'll see. I'm more than ready now. I'm twenty-two – in my prime – it's the ideal age according to some of the older women customers. We could start now, have a few years enjoying that one, then a year or two later, have another for company for it, before we are thirty. We would still be young enough and have enough energy to keep up with them as they grow. You wouldn't want an only child, would you?"

He had turned his back on her and lay quietly fuming. She leaned over his shoulder. "I bet you would have loved a little brother or sister to play with when you were little, wouldn't you? Be honest now!"

He turned abruptly back to face her, pushing her away with his arm.

"No, I bloody wouldn't have! And you've been discussing all this with bloody customers? Strangers hearing all our private business? What else have you been saying about me, I wonder!"

His face was thunderous. She was frightened. She had never seen this side of him before. She rushed to reassure him.

"No, of course not! I would never do that! It's just that some older wives talk about these things with us younger ones, about having babies and rearing children. It plays a big part in a woman's life, after all."

"You want to turn out like your mother, do you? Is that

your ambition? Is that what you want out of life? To be a fat, useless slob of a woman by the time you reach middle age, with a houseful of kids and no money? Well, that's not what I want! Get yourself a dog or a cat or something to satisfy your flaming broodiness and your ticking!"

"God!" Margaret was shocked, hurt and terrified by this vicious outburst.

"Let's get this straight now, Maggs, for once and for all. There will be no kids in this house, not now, not ever, not if I can help it. I do not want kids! Got it?"

Margaret was sobbing helplessly while this tirade was shouted at her. She reached out to him: "Oh God, no! Don't say that! You can't mean that!" No children? Ever? Why? "But that's not natural! It's what marriage is for! All men want children of their own. What point is there in living otherwise?"

"Maybe I'm not like 'other men' then," he snarled, making a move to get out of the bed. She grabbed his sleeve pulling at it and pleading again.

"A son, God, imagine: a little fair-haired angel of a boy – your spitting image! You couldn't help but love him. I know you couldn't!"

"Oh, you know that, do you? Just like me, eh? And how do you know, how does anyone know how their kids will turn out? A little angel or a little devil? Which one was I then, hmm? People only see what you want them to see, they can't see inside you, can't see the real you, can they? Not if you don't want them to."

He seemed to be rambling now in his temper. What could he possibly mean by all that? It didn't make sense. 'People can't see inside you' – a strange reason to deny her a child. What was he afraid of? Something was troubling him, obviously. He had snatched his arm from her grasp and was getting dressed. Where was he going now, at this time of the night? He slammed the bedroom door behind him as he stormed out. Minutes later she heard the front door bang and the car start up. She sat on the edge of the bed, stunned by it all, shivering with cold and terror, breaking her heart, her mind going over and over some of the horrible and weird things he had shouted at her, trying hard to understand what he had been going on about. Those cruel remarks he had made about her mother – there was no call for that. Why was he being so nasty? Was it that he was afraid she would lose her looks and figure? She didn't think so! Anyway, she would be perfectly content with just two children – she would soon get back into shape, he'd have no reason to feel ashamed of her in any way. Her poor mother hadn't a choice in the matter. Things were different for women then – a 'houseful' being a common occurrence. They had no say in the matter, no control over what could happen. But her father obviously loved her more, if anything, not less. And what could he have meant about 'a little angel or a little devil'? Children were just children.

A thought suddenly struck her – was it the responsibility he couldn't face? Then another fast on its heels – could he be ill? Was that why he was so unpredictable, temperamental? He did suffer from nightmares at times, she knew, and they really disturbed him but discussion about them was impossible. He'd wake soaking with sweat murmuring words she couldn't quite grasp, but surely these would fade, given time. Was he feeling guilty somehow about his parents' deaths? Did he blame himself for them in some way, that he could have prevented them happening, somehow? Her mood changed to worry now. Should she risk mentioning it all to Dr Tilsbury in confidence? Or would that make everything even worse? Where could their marriage go from here? If he was ill, then it was her place to be there to support him through it – in sickness and in health as her wedding vows said.

She must have sat there on the edge of the bed for hours, the eiderdown pulled around her, her thoughts and moods swinging from one extreme to the other – from anger to pity, from love to hate. It was beginning to get light. She looked at the clock. Seven o'clock. Where was he now? She got up and dressed.

January, a new year beginning. All hopes of a new beginning for their relationship dashed. It was Sunday. At least she didn't have to go to work in this condition, she was in no fit state to deal with or meet anyone. Half-heartedly she began tidying up and making the bed. Anything was better than just sitting there. She was putting the finishing touches to the room when her eyes fell on the packet on his bedside table. She stood and stared at them, her anger rising. She picked them up and opened the small drawer intending to put them out of her sight. Those things, those bloody things! They were the cause of all her misery. Venom coursed through her veins. She threw them onto the bed as if they were red hot and burned her fingers. She marched to the dressing table, grabbed a long hatpin and, holding it like a dagger, returned and stabbed at the packet again and again, picked it up, threw it in the drawer out of her sight and slammed it shut.

She didn't see Godfrey again until Monday dinner-time. She had gone to work as usual, unable to let the staff down without warning. During the morning a few of Godfrey's customers had come across to enquire as to why the shop hadn't opened. Where was he, they asked. *I wish I knew*, she thought, but as usual she covered up for him with the same excuses – "He had some business to attend to. He's still finding it hard at times, getting everything done. His father always saw to everything." And as usual, they grudgingly accepted her explanation.

At one o'clock she hurried home. There was no sign of the car. She made herself a cup of tea and a sandwich, though she had no appetite. She was about to force herself to eat it when he breezed in, his behaviour back to normal as if nothing had happened.

"Make us some food, Maggs, I'm starving!"

"Where have you been?" she said angrily.

"Shopping!"

She couldn't believe what she was hearing.

"Shopping! All day Sunday, when nowhere is open!" She tried hard to keep her anger under control – she didn't want him flaring up again. He seemed to be full of the joys of spring at the moment but one never knew with him.

"I've got a surprise for you. I'll show you after."

A surprise for her? What now? What next? Trying to stay calm, in control of her emotions and taking one tentative step at a time, she fried some eggs and bacon for him.

He finished his meal, got up from the table, took her hand and led her to the front door, throwing it wide open.

"There! What do you think of that, then? Isn't she beautiful? Oh, I've always wanted one of those and now I've got one. Eat your heart out, Dudley Bowen!"

A new, black MG stood in the road outside their house. There was no sign of the Austin Seven. So this was 'her' surprise!

He winked at her. "I might take you for a spin in it later, if you're a good girl!"

She was spinning enough as it was. "Where did you get that? We can't afford that, can we?"

"It's all bought and paid for. A mate of mine had a poker game going yesterday and I won. I put the old Austin in part-exchange, wrote a cheque and paid cash for the rest."

Easy come, easy go. So he was gambling now. "Wouldn't it have been better to wait a bit, God? The business can't be doing all that well at the moment, with the time you've been taking off."

She had gone too far, overstepped the mark. He grabbed her arm and swung her round to him, his face inches from hers.

"That 'business' is my business," he growled through clenched teeth, "it's nothing to do with you and it's none of your business what I do with it!" He pointed his finger in her face: "And don't you dare start preaching to me about money, I took enough of that from my bloody father! I won't take it from you!"

He was off again into a vile vicious mood. His own poor father the butt of his hatred now. If anyone was to hear those words, what would they think? Some of his rantings on Saturday night flashed across her mind: "People see only what you want them to see… they can't see inside you, can they?" Scared stiff but not sure of what again, she turned and went back to the kitchen, grabbed her coat and bag and left by the back door to return to work. It was easier to walk away from trouble than stay and confront it, she had found. Her mind raced as she walked, full to bursting point again of questions that had no answers. She never knew he gambled. How much had he won? How much was his stake? And how many times had he lost, prior to winning? They could lose everything overnight with a game like poker. She had seen that happen in films… a dangerous game involving dangerous people! Fortunes were lost far more often than fortunes were won. In many cases it became addictive, destroying families, ruining lives.

CHAPTER 18

A Chance Discovery

FOUR MONTHS HAD passed, life for the two of them carrying on much as before, both of them continuing to cover up the strained atmosphere whenever they were in company. These days they spent very little time together on their own. It suited Margaret and she knew it suited Godfrey. They still slept together but that was all that took place in their bed. She was glad of that, too. They were living more or less separate lives now.

It was April, a Sunday morning and a beautiful spring day. Godfrey had got up early and gone to the shop. He usually did now on a Sunday morning – he must be getting short of cash, thought his wife. She had gone back to sleep enjoying his absence from the bed – a deep, relaxing sleep for the first time for ages. These last few months had passed without incident, thank goodness. Ever the optimist, Margaret still clung to the hope that maybe, just maybe, now that he had what he 'always wanted' – that damned car – they might have gone through the worst and reached a turning point. That's what her heart hoped. Despite everything, she still had feelings for him. Her head told her: wishful thinking – wake up to reality!

She got up and stretched, the sunlight streaming into the bedroom lifting her spirits. A perfect day for spending in the garden, she thought. The spring bulbs were poking through. There was a lot of tidying up to be done to see them at their best. She looked at her fingernails. They needed filing before she started. She hated wearing gloves in the garden, preferring to touch the leaves and flowers, marvelling always at the endless variety, the colours and the designs. She opened the drawer in her bedside table looking for her nail file. It wasn't there. Godfrey must have borrowed it. He never put anything back after him. She walked round and opened his drawer, the memory of the punctured packet coming instantly to mind. It wasn't there! She rummaged about, finding the file but not the packet. She jumped to a conclusion again. Had he changed his mind, got rid of them? She tried to hold on to the thought as she began filing her nails but it evaporated as quickly as it had materialised.

Armed with her gardening tools and kneeling pad she went out into the back garden, resigned to her circumstances but determined to get pleasure out of her life wherever she could. Gardening was one of her main sources. Time passed quickly and she soon reached the border at the top of the lawn. Kneeling by a Rose of Sharon bush, she gently brushed to one side the decaying debris beneath it to reveal a large patch of crocuses already in bud. They were beautiful: white, blue, yellow and mauve on the point of bursting open once the sun touched them. She sat back on her heels looking at them and enjoying them. A movement in the lane distracted her. She leaned forward and peeped through the fence palings. Oh, it was that pretty Mrs Polinski – Isabel – the lawyer's wife from further up the street.

Margaret was about to rise and say good morning when something about her behaviour stopped her. Isabel was looking furtively about as she moved to the dry-stone wall on the other side of the lane. Satisfied that there was no-one about, she quickly removed a stone, took out a piece of paper, replaced it with one from her pocket and put the stone back on top. Strange! With another quick look around she turned and retraced her steps up the lane to her house.

Margaret remained where she was, not moving a muscle, intrigued by what she had witnessed. What was that all about? Her curiosity got the better of her. She walked to the garden gate, leaned over it and looked up and down the lane. There was no-one in sight. She scampered across to the wall, took out the note, read it, replaced it and scampered back, walking quickly down the path and into the kitchen. The words on the note had been few, but shocking: "I'm pregnant. Must see you." See who? Oh no! The thoughts were leaping into her mind. Not Godfrey! No! He couldn't do that: deprive her of her heart's desire only to make another man's wife the mother of his child. That was too cruel, surely, even for him! Then why was the note opposite their garden? Questions, questions: always questions and never any answers. She had to find out the truth this time – all of it.

Feverishly she scrubbed at her nails and began preparing their dinner, her mind frantically trying to work out a plan. Going by the routine of the last few weeks, Godfrey should be home around three for his meal, usually followed by a nap in the chair, then a bath and change, and off in his MG for a night on the town somewhere with his mates. He never took that car to the shop – he always walked there and back. The next thought hit her like a sledgehammer: on Sundays and only on Sundays, he came and went by the back lane! Now she knew why. Now she was certain she was right: it was him!

At ten minutes to three their dinners were dished up and ready. Covering them with saucepan lids she placed them in the oven and went upstairs into the back bedroom. From there she could see clearly, through the net curtain, into the lane. The minutes passed, her eyes not moving, hardly blinking. There he was, at the start of their fence! Would he cross to the wall or open the gate? With her heart in her mouth, she watched but she already knew the answer before he was halfway along.

Yes. The wall. The note was removed and read, crumpled and put in his pocket. After a quick glance around, he took out his diary and a biro, scribbled something, ripped out a sheet and inserted it behind the stone. Margaret sank to her knees with a low moan, her whole body limp, deflated.

"Margaret? Where are you? Is dinner ready?" She jumped at the sound of his voice. Scrambling to her feet and pulling herself together, she shouted back: "Yes. I'll be there now. I'm in the bathroom." She took a deep breath and walked downstairs.

Dinner over, Godfrey settled in the armchair to glance through the Sunday papers while she cleared the table, washed the dishes and waited for him to drop off to sleep, as he usually did. Her jobs all finished, he was still wide awake. Too much on his mind, she mused wryly.

She had to get up there, see what the note said before he went out again and before Isabel turned up to collect it. She might even have done so by now and be getting ready to meet him somewhere. She was on pins, waiting. The newspapers were dropped to the floor. He was getting up. Automatically she bent to pick up and fold the papers.

"Is the water hot?"

She nodded.

"Right. I'm off for a bath."

"I'll be up the garden finishing off, if there's anything you want."

"Have you ironed my shirt?"

"The blue one? Yes." It was his favourite. "It's on the bed."

They went their separate ways, he to the bathroom, she to the top of the garden. She was safe enough to investigate: he wouldn't see her. The only place he could see her from was his parents' bedroom and he avoided that like the plague. Within minutes the deed was done – the note retrieved, read and replaced: "Meet tomorrow, 1.15 park seat on left by azalea tree." Margaret would be there too, hidden and waiting.

At one o'clock she left the Cop, her sandwiches and a *Woman's Own* magazine in her bag. She wouldn't be lunching with the staff today, she said – she was meeting Pauline. They would be none the wiser. She had developed into a good liar. Another fine, warm day – providence must be on her side. She walked, unrushed, to the park. It wasn't far – she was there in five minutes. She walked on the path behind the azalea tree, pausing, apparently, to admire the abundance of huge mauve flowers it bore but, in reality, checking that she couldn't be seen from the seat on the other side.

She settled herself on the grass and checked again from this angle. Other lime-hating bushes were growing around the base of the tree, allowing enough vision for her to see who approached but sufficient cover to pass unnoticed herself. She opened her bag and took out the sandwiches and her magazine, not that she wanted to eat or read. They were merely props for her subterfuge, should anyone pass by. Heaven forbid that it would be someone she knew! Taking a nibble from her ham sandwich and turning a page she suddenly saw the funny side of the ridiculous situation she found herself in. It was just like a film, She was an undercover detective, a sleuth, a private eye, gathering important information! She smiled. Then the reality of what she was actually doing wiped it away. Her husband was meeting another man's wife whom he had made pregnant with a child she had wanted so much but been refused. This was the last straw. There would be no going back from here but she would finish it in her own time. She would see him humiliated first, make him suffer!

There were footsteps approaching on the other path, high heels clacking on the tarmac. They stopped by the seat. Margaret peeped through the bushes. It was Isabel. Sitting in one corner of it, she too took out a packet of sandwiches and a magazine. Godfrey turned up soon afterwards and occupied the opposite end of the seat. He opened a newspaper, held it up in front of his face and immediately began talking in a low voice. Margaret could hear his every word.

"It's not mine! It can't be. I always take care."

Isabel answered calmly: "It is yours, Godfrey. It must have been faulty."

Margaret put her hand over her mouth as she drew in her breath, flashes of her frantic stabbing with her hatpin passing before her eyes. It was through her that this had happened! She struggled to concentrate again, each word even more significant to her now. Isabel was talking again. She didn't seem to be in the least bothered about her predicament, by the sound of her voice.

"I knew it would happen sooner or later, God: either an accident or you would turn up empty-handed and take the risk. It's what I wanted to happen, what I had planned."

Godfrey was getting angry, his voice getting more aggressive. "I tell you it's not mine – it can't be mine. It's your husband's!" His mouth twisted as he added "Or someone else's!"

"How dare you! Someone else's? What do you take me

for? I'm not one of your fancy women!" The next three words were said slowly and deliberately. "It is yours."

"How do you know that? How can you be so sure?"

"Oh, I know. You see, this was all planned from the beginning by me and my husband!"

Godfrey was astounded. So was Margaret.

"Planned?"

"Yes, planned." She giggled. "You didn't think I fell in love with you, did you Godfrey? You silly man. What would be the point? You can only ever love yourself. No, we were just using you. My husband is the only man I will ever love and I would willingly die for him. But you see, he can't have children. He spent his war years in a concentration camp. He is infertile as a result of all he suffered there. He longs for a child – as I do."

She looked down at her tummy and caressed it.

"You and your seductive charm were the answer to our prayers. You have our colouring, you see: same fair hair, same colour eyes, same complexion. Adopted babies grow up adopting their new parents' mannerisms – did you know that? It will be ours in every sense of the word."

She lifted her eyes and looked at him. "We are both extremely happy, thanks to you Godfrey. We thought it only fair for you to know the truth – the reason why I'm dumping you. You are no longer needed. We also know it will go no further. You wouldn't want that lovely wife of yours to hear of your adultery, would you? I do feel guilty about that but if I hadn't come along, someone else would have, wouldn't they?"

Margaret couldn't believe all she was hearing. She could understand what it was like to long for a baby, to have that nagging ache in the pit of your stomach that never went away – but to go that far? And with her husband's full co-operation? She moved her position to get a better view of Godfrey's face. He was seething with anger, she could see. Crumpling his newspaper and tossing it aside, he leaned towards her. His voice, low and menacing, forced through clenched teeth sent a chill through her body.

"You get rid of it! You hear me? Get rid of it. I don't want kids. I won't have kids. I can't!"

There they were again – those same words he had spat out at her. Isabel was unperturbed.

"Oh but you can, Godfrey, obviously." She caressed her tummy again lovingly, tenderly and smiling as she did so.

"You don't get it, do you?"

Neither do I, thought Margaret. Would he enlighten them both now, she wondered.

"You don't know what you're doing, what you're in for, how it will turn out, you stupid bitch! You can't have my kid – I won't let you!" His words were coming thick and fast, his body getting more and more agitated. "Get rid of it! I'll pay. Use someone else for your dirty little scheme!" He rose now and stood in front of her poking his finger menacingly close to her face. "You get rid of it, or else…"

"Just what are you afraid of Godfrey – that it will turn out like you? Oh, there's no fear of that, I can assure you!" She almost laughed, "And 'or else' what?"

"Or else be careful. Be very careful. You could have a nasty accident that might get rid of it for you!"

Mrs Polinski laughed out loud. How could that woman be so calm?

"Are you threatening me, Godfrey?"

"No, just warning you as to what could happen, if you don't do what I say."

"Murder your own child? That's preposterous!" She was deadly serious. "I think you need help Godfrey, you are a very sick man!" She got up casually and gathered her things together, then added with a grin: "And perhaps just a little bit over-dramatic. Goodbye Godfrey!" She walked away without looking back.

Now he was getting up, swearing to himself – Margaret heard the word 'bitch' several times – and headed off in the opposite direction. She had sat with her knuckles in her mouth, biting down hard on them during most of the conversation that took place on the bench. She kept her eyes on her husband until he had passed out of sight, then put his paper, her magazine and her sandwiches in a bin and went to sit on the seat herself until she heard the village clock strike a quarter to two.

The afternoon shift in the Cop passed in a haze. Mondays were usually quiet, customers popping in for just one or two items. Moira and Wilf mostly did the serving while the three girls got on with the cleaning, filling the fixtures and weighing provisions. Margaret opted for the cleaning, finding it much easier to be alone with her thoughts as she polished windows, swept floors and scrubbed counters, than making conversation with Joan and Sarah. She was in no mood for their banter – she wouldn't be able to concentrate and join in. Her head was whirling with all she'd heard. This was definitely the last straw now. He would pay for this. She would see he would. Her marriage was dead, she finally accepted it had all been a huge mistake. Why hadn't she realised it before? She'd had her doubts, why hadn't she taken more notice of them? Isabel had seen through him straight away and she was right – the only person he could ever love was himself. Why hadn't she seen that, too? She was too wrapped up in her feelings for him: that was why. Well, she was well and truly over that now. But she would get her revenge first – and take her time doing it.

Later that evening, their meal finished, she asked, "Are you going out tonight?"

"Yeh, down the pub with Dudley. Why?"

"Just asking." She wanted the house to herself. There was something she needed to do – to put a cat among his pigeons, so to speak!

By eight o'clock he had gone; she switched off the TV, returned to the kitchen, took a pad, pen and envelope from the dresser drawer and sat by the table. She printed out an address on the envelope first – To: Mr Alec Polinski, 24 Fair View, Lower Crymceynon.

In the top left-hand corner she printed 'Private' and in the bottom right-hand corner she printed 'Local'. Next, she wrote out a short note in the middle of a sheet of writing paper: "I know your wife is pregnant and the baby she is carrying is not yours."

She folded it, placed it in the envelope, sealed it and stuck on a stamp. Putting on her coat, she slipped out of the house and walked to the nearest postbox. She dropped the letter in. It landed with a quiet little plop. It would cause a big bang soon!

CHAPTER 19

Second Thoughts

TUESDAY MORNING. GODFREY ate his breakfast with a preoccupied look on his face throughout and not a happy one. Just wait, Margaret told herself, be patient. The letter might well arrive today by the afternoon post. Ones marked 'local' usually did. She actually hummed to herself as she got ready for work, picturing the letter's arrival. Of course, Mr Polinski knew he wasn't the father and knew who was but no-one else should know. He would jump to the conclusion that Godfrey had blabbed about it, bragged to someone about his conquest with the lawyer's wife – a feather in his cap.

Mr Polinski was a decent, well-respected man of principle but his wife's reputation was at stake here. The wife he adored and who adored him. Godfrey would suffer some justice at his hands. She couldn't help but feel sorry for involving the Polinskis, having heard their history. She never thought she was capable of harbouring such spite and hatred without even considering what the consequences might be. These feelings were foreign to her. Godfrey was to blame for that, for this change in her. Now that she looked at the wider picture of what she had done. she was beginning to regret it and worry about it. If she could relive the last twenty-four hours, would she still have sent the letter? But it was too late, it was done. What was happening to her, what type of a person was she becoming? A liar, a schemer, a sneak! But she hadn't asked for any of this. None of this was her fault, was it? All she had done was fall madly and blindly in love with Godfrey. There was no love left now. Her hate had fed on it till it had all gone. She pressed her hands against the sides of her skull – all this torment, all the time. One thing after another. Would she ever achieve peace of mind again?

At half past seven that evening, she was sitting tensely in the front room away from her husband. She couldn't even bear to sit in the same room with him for long. She heard him pass the door and climb the stairs – to get ready to go out again.

The door bell rang. She knew who it would be before she opened it. The letter had arrived. Trembling inside and struggling to compose herself, she lifted the latch and trying to look surprised she said, "Oh, Mr Polinski! Come in."

"Good evening, Mrs Parson. Er, is your husband in by any chance? I'd like to have a word with him, if he is."

"Um, yes. He's upstairs, I'll give him a shout. Come in." She led the way to the front room, invited him to sit down and went to the foot of the stairs. "Godfrey!" she shouted, "It's someone to see you. Can you come down?"

She didn't mention who it was – he would find out soon enough and she wanted to watch his reaction when he did. She heard the toilet flush and in a moment or two down he came. She walked in front of him, pausing by the door to let him pass. When he saw who it was he took an involuntary step backwards, bumping into her. Alec Polinski moved forward smiling, his hand stretched out in greeting, his bearing dignified and polite.

"Evening Mr Parson," he said, shaking his hand, "I'm sorry to bother you but could I just have a word?" He leaned forward and lowered his voice. "In private!"

Godfrey's body was giving out signals. He was extremely nervous. Those two words, though gently spoken, carried a menacing message. "Certainly." He turned to his wife and muttered, "Business, it's about business," motioning her to leave with a curt jerk of his head towards the door.

Alec smiled across at her. "I won't keep him long, Mrs Parson, I promise." She smiled back, thinking *Take as long as you like*, then glanced again at Godfrey's scared face before leaving and closing the door, but not tightly, behind her. She hovered in the passage, listening.

Alec spoke first, authoritatively. "Sit down and listen. Carefully."

Godfrey sat and looked up at this big, quietly spoken man, who seemed much bigger suddenly, standing over him. He shrank back in his chair.

"I know it was you who made my wife pregnant – as she told you, we had planned it. But today I received an anonymous letter from someone else who knows. That knowledge could only have come from you."

Godfrey tried to protest his innocence but Alec held up his hand.

"Whoever it is that you boasted to, you will get in touch with and deny it. Convincingly."

Godfrey was shaking his head, vigorously. "But I haven't! Honest to God, Alec, I haven't! What do you take me for? Would I brag about a thing like that? My own wife could get to hear of it!"

"The answer to your questions are – one, a total bastard and two, yes, you would. You have told someone, one of your degenerate associates, no doubt. Now, you sort it because if I hear just one besmirching my wife's good character I can assure you I will destroy you. I'm a lawyer, as you know, well acquainted with people of importance and influence, including the police..."

Godfrey flinched, Alec moved closer and emphasised each word of what he said next: "This baby my wife is carrying is ours. Not yours. Ours. It will be loved, cared for and cherished…"

Godfrey butted in. "But you don't understand! You can't! It must…"

"Oh yes, we can and we will. And if you come within a mile of my wife with your bullying and your pathetic threats…" his face was very close to Godfrey's, "you won't know what's hit you!"

He straightened up and moved to the door. His hand on the handle, he turned and spoke again. "Oh, for your information, we will be moving from the area before the baby is born to begin our new life as a complete family and for the sake of your lovely wife. She doesn't deserve a spineless control freak like you!"

He paused, considering, and raising his eyebrows.

"Perhaps it would be best if we were to tell her though, before we leave – let her know what a waster she married – if she doesn't know already! I'll let myself out."

Margaret flew back towards the kitchen.

"Goodnight, Mr Parson," then, in a quieter voice: "Goodnight, Mrs Parson," as he spotted her in mid-flight.

When the front door had closed she returned to the front room, seemingly to switch on the television, and asked casually: "Was the 'business' sorted alright?"

Godfrey was deep in thought. "Mm? Oh, Alec. Yes. He wanted to know if I could keep him some nice steak for this weekend."

"Oh, was that all!"

"Mm. He wants to cook a special meal for them both. His wife has just told him that she's pregnant."

"Really? That's nice for them."

Godfrey didn't answer.

Tomorrow, she decided, she would call to the Polinski's house and explain about that letter, tell them everything. She didn't want them to worry and she knew instinctively that she could trust them with all she would tell them.

Chapter 20

Letters between Friends

The schools were breaking up for the long summer holidays. Pauline would have about six weeks off. Margaret longed to see her. She had such a lot she wanted to talk to her about. She would write and ask her when she'd be coming to Crymceynon next, on a visit. To ask her to come and stay at Fairview was still out of the question but at least they could spend the best part of one or more days together. Margaret intended telling her everything now, every last detail, and of her intention to divorce Godfrey, but not in a letter. All she had to say would never fit in the envelope!

She began: "Dear Pauline, I apologise before you read through this letter, for loading you with all my troubles. There is no-one here I can confide in, not even my own mother as yet, but I will soon. I am at my wits' end not knowing where to turn just now. I need to confess to you first, the truth, at last, of my sham of a marriage. I knew on my wedding day, the moment you had all gone home, that very first night, that I had made such a big mistake. But it will take a whole book not a few pages from a writing pad to explain how I've got to where I am. It's enough to say I've come to my senses at last, and it's over, or at least coming to an end very soon. It has to now. I have been such a gullible fool from day one. The more I look back, seeing it all in perspective, the more I realise how he has used and manipulated me. Perhaps I'm beginning to get paranoid at some of the conclusions I am reaching. I have serious doubts, now that I know the real him, even about his parents' accidents! No proof of course – no-one else has ever doubted that they were accidents, including the police. But he's responsible somehow, I feel it. Perhaps they, like me, had discovered the real Godfrey: that their idol of a son had feet of clay and couldn't bear to live with the thought of other people finding out! See? I said paranoid, didn't I?

"I desperately need to talk to you, to hear your opinion and seek your help and advice. Things have been going round my head so much I just can't make head or tail of them anymore. To be honest, I'm worried about my own state of mind, Pol. I'm so sorry to be burdening you with all this in a letter. I just need to know if you can come, and when. He is out most of the time and spends less and less time at the shop. Sales are plummeting. Customers in the Cop keep asking why is it shut so often and what is the matter. All I can say is 'business troubles'. If you can come Pol, any Sunday would be the best day to call – around dinner-time would be fine. He's always gone by mid-morning, sometimes even sooner. Sometimes from the evening before!

"Don't say much in your reply, Pol, in case he opens it by mistake, or deliberately! I'm sorry my letter is so muddled. Please write soon. Your loving friend, Marg."

Pauline wrote by return, a short note but to the point. She would be in Crymceynon on the following Saturday and would see her on the Sunday about half past eleven. If the weather was fine they could cut some sandwiches and go for a nice long walk up the mountain. The fresh air and exercise would do them both good – blow some cobwebs away!

Pauline's first port of call, always, on coming home, was to the bottom of Duke Street, to her grandparents. Gran would be expecting her, with a tray of refreshments set out ready. She usually stopped for about an hour before that final little climb with her suitcase to the top of Stephen's Street. Carrie was on the doorstep, looking out for her as she turned the corner from Parry's Terrace. She gave Pauline a little wave then disappeared back inside to wet the tea. For the first quarter of an hour she avoided mentioning her friend's name, though she urgently wanted to find out what, if anything, Carrie had heard. To her surprise it was Carrie who brought the subject up.

"Have you heard from Margaret Pierce at all lately?" sipping her tea and trying to sound casual as she asked.

"Yes, I had a long letter from her a few days ago."

Carrie replaced her cup in the saucer and folded her arms on the table, leaning forward, her expression hesitant and undecided. Pauline leaned forward too, determined to coax it all out of her.

"I'm bound to tell you, Pol! I'm very worried about that girl. She doesn't look at all well these days. I'm sure it's down to that husband of hers."

There! Pol knew it – Gran had never liked him for some reason, whatever that was. She couldn't even bring herself to mention his name.

"You don't like him, do you? You know something, don't you? What is it, Gran? Tell me please! I've had a letter from her that is worrying me to bits."

Carrie hesitated but only for a few seconds. Yes, she decided, with a firm nod to herself: it was right that Pauline should know.

"That man has gone to the dogs, good and proper. Literally, too – he'll bet on anything! Gambling, drinking and what not. Oh, a few have seen him in the town – in Cardiff too – with some bright looking sparks and not only men!"

Carrie paused, not sure how much she should say. Pauline nodded encouragingly.

"He can't blame any of this behaviour on losing his parents, can he, and expect sympathy? That money has gone to his head. Margaret sees none of it, I can tell you – he's never out with her! And the business is going downhill, fast. All that hard work his parents and grandparents put in, running away like water in his hands. Nothing but the best for him – clothes, jewellery, a posh, sporty kind of car…"

Carrie lifted both hands despairingly and let them drop back in her lap, getting upset by it all. "Go and see her, Pol, as soon as you can. She doesn't deserve this. Make her see sense. No-one will blame her. She should never have married him."

She rose from her chair, taking the teapot to the kettle to add more water, muttering under her breath: "I wish I had said something then, at the time, but how could I? I was too confused and Albert said…"

Pauline heard snatches of what she was saying. Startled, she rose too and went after her. "What was that Gran? Say that again."

Carrie looked up, surprised, unaware that she had voiced her thoughts. "Say what?"

"That you wished you had said something before but couldn't and something about Grampa."

Flummoxed and frightened, Carrie waved her hand at her granddaughter. "It was nothing. My imagination, that's all." She gave a big sigh and sat down again. "Anyway, it's far too late now."

"For goodness sake, Gran! Too late for what? It isn't 'nothing', is it? You heard something, saw something, didn't you? What, when? Tell me!"

The look on Carrie's face was pitiful. She looked as if she was about to burst into tears with this scolding from her grandchild. Pauline grabbed her handbag from the table and took out Margaret's letter, handed it to her and ordered her, "Read that!"

Carrie took it and read, taking her time while Pauline watched her closely. The silence was interrupted several times with sporadic one-word exclamations from Carrie, her hand flying to her mouth with each one. When she had finished reading it she slapped the letter down in her lap, triumphantly.

"There! I knew it! I knew I was right!"

"What did you know, Gran? Please! You must tell me!"

Carrie opened her mouth then closed it again, still reluctant. Her eyes fastened beseechingly on Pauline's face before she began.

"You can't repeat any of what I tell you now, Pol. Not one word mind, not to anybody. Understand? The only person I ever told was Grampa. He convinced me it meant nothing. He explained it all and I believed it. Well, I wanted to believe it. But Albert wasn't there: he didn't see what I saw. It just wouldn't go away!"

Bit by bit Carrie went over the whole of that terrible morning back in June 1952. The date was imprinted on her memory – Friday the thirteenth – everything as clear in her mind now as it was then. When she had finished she begged Pauline again: "You promise me, mind. You can't mention this to anyone!"

"But Gran, the police should know!"

"Know what – that he smiled? We could still be jumping to conclusions. What Albert said could be the true explanation, couldn't it? The police found absolutely no evidence of a crime being committed in either case – nothing. Perhaps what Margaret suspects is the truth – that his behaviour drove them to it. After all, as Albert says: what does a smile prove?"

This information shed a new light on everything for Pauline but failed to enlighten her as what to believe. One thing she was sure of though.

"She can't stay there. Not now, she can't. I'll take her back with me. I'll explain to my flatmates that her marriage is breaking up and she has to get away. They won't mind I'm sure. We'll manage for a week or two till we can make some other arrangements. We'll work something out. But she is not staying there with him!"

Chapter 21

Finders, Keepers

Margaret was up and about early on Sunday morning. Godfrey had already left. He wouldn't be home again until the early hours of Monday. Great! Pauline was due to call later and she was so looking forward to it. Six o'clock now: five and a half hours before she'd arrive. What could she do to make the time pass quicker? She'd find something. Bathed and dressed, she tidied the bedroom and bathroom and was on her way downstairs when she noticed, not for the first time, how worn the stair carpet was on the edges of some of the steps. The top three on the bend, where the carpet was fitted, were fine but the further down you went, the worse they were. Sooner or later someone could trip on those and have a nasty fall. She'd have to remember to warn Pauline about them – those high heels she wore could easily catch and she could go flying! The more she thought about it, the more dangerous they looked. She looked closer. It would only be a matter of lifting the clips on either side and turning it top to bottom; the worn part would be against the risers then and the better part on the steps. It wouldn't look very nice but she wouldn't be there to look at it much longer. Mm. It would pass the time. Breakfast first and a read through the newspaper and she'd do it. The sun shone brightly through the fanlights of the front and porch doors. She opened both of them wide, and stood on the doorstep with her face to the sun and her eyes closed. A day like today couldn't fail to lift one's spirits. She walked back to the kitchen carrying her paper and milk bottles and leaving both doors wide open behind her.

Her breakfast finished, she hunted in the cwtch under the stairs for the toolbox, found it and carried it to the foot of the staircase. The first few pairs of clips lifted up quite easily but got stiffer the higher up she went, the last pair being the tightest of all. Well, she had come this far – she wouldn't give up now! Ah! At last, it was free. Going carefully back to the bottom, she pulled and rolled the carpet and stacked it on one side. With her hands on her hips, she looked upwards at the bare flight, feeling very satisfied with her achievement. She needn't bother to put the damn thing back – why should she? Her only reason for removing it was for Pauline's safety. Let Godfrey struggle with it. Back in the kitchen, she washed her hands, filled the kettle and looked at the clock. Just ten minutes to ten – nearly two hours more to fill before she would see her friend.

Pauline hadn't slept much through the night, fretting over the long conversation she'd had with her Gran yesterday and worrying about her friend's safety. At seven o'clock she had made up her mind. To hell with Godfrey, if he was there or not! She was going over there to bring her back. By nine-thirty, loaded with a picnic basket and in flat shoes for mountain climbing, she was on her way to Fair View.

Seeing the two front doors wide open, she hurried up the path and walked straight through to the passage, shouting her name – "Margaret? Where are you? Are you OK?"

She came running from the kitchen at the sound of Pauline's voice. "Pol!" They hugged in greeting. "You're early! I wasn't expecting you till half-eleven!

"Well, I'll wait outside till then, is it?" Laughter between them already – they were both going to make the most of these hours together. She lifted her basket: "Fancy a picnic?"

"Yeh, up on the top of the mountain! I haven't been up there for years!"

"And we used to practically live up there when we were little. Happy days eh, Marg?"

"Mm, happy days." For a moment her face clouded over. She shook back her hair, determined to look forward not back. "Hey, you've got flat shoes on! And there's me taking the stair-carpet off so you don't catch your high heels in the worn bits!"

"More fool you!" Laughter again. It felt good. "Kettle's boiled. Let's have a coffee and then we'll be off."

"Where's he?" asked Pauline.

"I don't know and I don't care," she replied, laying their cups before them on the table. Pauline was sitting opposite the still open cwtch door, staring into the darkness – a black hole. It seemed to symbolise her friend's marriage somehow. Wait! There was light in there, little specks of light, twinkling and sparkling. She must be imagining it – they had gone again.

As she sipped her coffee, she wondered how best to go about the conversation that would soon develop and thinking of what Carrie had told her in confidence, yesterday.

She couldn't repeat any of it to her friend – a promise was a promise. Besides, Margaret had enough on her plate to confuse and worry her as it was. But she was absolutely determined to persuade her to leave him now, she would not leave this house without her in tow. A silence had fallen between them. Pauline waited patiently for Margaret to break it, sipping her drink and nibbling at a biscuit.

It wasn't long before the silence cracked – slowly at first, then suddenly into lots of tiny pieces that Pauline tried to fix together.

"I knew that first evening Pol, after you had all gone. He didn't love me. He never had and never would no matter how hard I tried to make him." She related that first night in detail. "The only feeling he had was lust and even that soon began to wane. He has done only what Godfrey wants to do, all along, in everything. Nothing and no-one else matters to him, only his own needs and requirements."

She had put up with his absences at weekends, not knowing where he was, who he was with or what he was doing and he never enlightened her. Then there was the drinking and gambling, the money disappearing rapidly, not only on horses and dogs, which was bad enough, but private games of poker.

"He waltzed in one day with a brand new MG, bragging that he had won a lot on cards, put the Austin in part-exchange and casually written a cheque for the rest! What were the stakes for that game? And how many times had he lost sums like that? More times than he had won, that's for sure."

She broke down when she related what had led up to that event – the night she had broached the subject of starting a family – "My last and only hope of making my marriage tolerable"– and how he had been so cruel about her mother.

"He didn't want *kids*, he said, he wouldn't have *kids*, he couldn't have *kids*!" Margaret hated that word for children and emphasised it every time she said it. Kids were young goats, children were young human beings. "He said you could never tell how they would turn out."

"That's a strange thing to say. What sort of reason is that?"

"Yes, and he said exactly the same words to Isabel Polinski!"

"Who?"

"The woman he had an affair with. Well, one of many, I found out later."

"Oh no! Oh, Marg!"

By the time Margaret had related all of that episode and the part she had played in it, the tears were streaming down her face.

"Get rid of it, he told her! He was prepared to murder his own child, Pol! How could he say such a thing?"

Oh, quite easily, thought Pauline staring ahead into the darkness of the cwtch again, picturing all her friend had borne, forced to keep everything to herself, all this time. She had no idea things had been as bad as this. She leaned forward and reached out her hands to clasp hers.

"Oh, Marg!" This would end today, Her friend had suffered more than enough. Margaret was sitting with her back to the cwtch and the darkness behind her brightened a little as the sun came out from behind a passing cloud. The twinklings and sparklings were back in there again! What were they? She rose quickly to investigate before they disappeared once more.

Margaret wrapped in her misery looked up, not understanding this sudden withdrawal of Pol's. Was she going on a bit too much? Was Pauline fed up with all her moaning?

"I'm sorry Pol, rabbiting on all the time spoiling your visit. It's just that it's such a relief to be able to unload it at..."

She hastened to reassure her friend. "No, Marg, no, it's not that love, of course it isn't! I want, need, to know every last detail. No, it's something in there, in the cwtch, shining now and then and catching my eye. I wondered what it was. Come and see. There, look! And there! It's all over the place if you move your head about a bit."

The sun was at its height now, flooding through the open front doors and forcing its rays through the slits in the bare staircase. Margaret tried to pinpoint where they were coming from and soon tracked them down. They were jammed in the narrow spaces between the stairs and the risers.

"It looks like there are rows of them," said Pauline. "What are they?"

"Well, we'll soon find out," said Margaret, hurrying to the cutlery drawer and taking out two knives. They stuck the blades straight in between the slits then turned them back towards themselves. Several bits fell to the floor with a metallic ring. Both girls bent to retrieve them, opened their hands to examine them then looked up at each other, wide grins spreading across their faces.

"Sovereigns!" they squealed in unison.

Quickly, the two girls cleared the cwtch floor and walls of its contents, searching through everything bit by bit – it wouldn't do for Godfrey to come across a stray one by accident. Obviously he was unaware of this hoard or it wouldn't be here, it would have long gone. Between them they examined every step, standing on chairs to reach the highest. The coins continued to shower out – music to their ears as they tinkled on the concrete.

Stacking them neatly on the kitchen table in little piles of ten, they added them up. Twenty little piles – two hundred sovereigns! They grabbed each other and danced a little jig. Then suddenly they stopped and stood staring at each other, flabbergasted, then burst into near-hysterical shrieks.

"You're free, Marg! You're free, girl, at last!" She stopped again, her finger on her lips. "The doors are open, he could walk in on us at any minute!"

Margaret, feeling slightly drunk with this sudden turn of

events concerning her future, waved away her friend's fears. "Oh, no need to worry about his Lordship. He won't be back!"

Pauline wasn't so sure. "Well, just in case. Let's get everything sorted."

The hoard, diligently saved by Godfrey's father and grandfather for the benefit of the following generations had finally been exposed. Pauline examined the coins closer.

"Get a pen and paper, Marg. These must be worth at least a couple of pounds each now, surely."

"What?!"

"Maybe even more. Look, they're all in excellent condition." She picked up a pile, turning them over in her hand. "There are some with Queen Victoria on, some with King Edward and some with King George V."

Margaret put the pen and paper on the table.

"Oh, and fetch a bag, Marg. Let's get them all out of sight first."

A handkerchief sachet was found and brought, the coins secreted inside it. Taking the dates and condition of the various coins into account, Pauline came up with a rough estimate as to the total value – under-estimated rather than over. She sucked in her breath as she drew a line under her final calculation and passed it to her friend. "Over a thousand pounds, Marg! You've got at least that and probably quite a bit more. A fortune!"

Margaret was chewing her bottom lip, having second thoughts. "Yes, but it's not mine, is it?" Her voice was low, resigned. "I can't take it, Pol."

"Bullshit!" said Pauline, shocking herself with her spontaneous outburst, the two of them giggling again, like a pair of naughty schoolgirls. "Of course you can! Listen, you are entitled to all of this – compensation for what he's put you through. Don't you dare turn your back on this one chance to rebuild your life. Finders, keepers, remember?"

"But what if Godfrey knows or worse still, finds out?"

"Bugger Godfrey!" More giggles. "See? See the effect that man has on people? I have never, ever sworn like this. Now it's twice in as many seconds! That man makes me so angry! And anyway, he can't know of their existence, can he? If he did he would have thrown most of it away on poker by now. Be honest – whose hands would poor old Esther and Gilbert prefer it to be in? Use your head, Marg – think straight!"

Margaret listened and had to agree with what her friend was saying. Her guilty feelings subsided. "You're right Pol. I'll see to it that none of it will be wasted."

"Of course you will. Now, never mind about mountain climbing – we'll have a quick cup of tea and some of those sandwiches I made and then we'll get that flaming carpet put back exactly the way it was. Then it's home for you, Marg – to your Mam's. You are not living here any longer. Right?"

"Right, Miss Bossyboots!" It was over now, finished and her Mam should be the first in Crymceynon to hear about it.

Walking home to Stephen's Street together, up the canal bank with each carrying a suitcase full of Margaret's belongings, they stopped now and again to rest and discuss what they would do next. First and foremost, no-one other than themselves must know of their treasure trove. Pauline would keep it with her, safe from Margaret's family's prying eyes. They would all want to help her with her unpacking, especially the youngsters. Secondly, when she returned to work tomorrow – for she had no intention of hiding away – she would explain to the staff what she had done and why, regarding her marriage, and apply for a week's holiday to be taken as soon as possible. During that week, both girls would return to Cardiff and spend the first few days getting rid of the sovereigns. They nearly came to blows during this discussion arguing over sharing out the spoils - Margaret insisting that Pauline should have half as it was she who had found it. Pauline was adamant that she wouldn't take a penny.

"Nonsense! No, I can't do that, Marg, honestly – it wouldn't be right. That money is yours to pick up the pieces and start again. Don't ask me, please."

"I'd still be there, wouldn't I, if it wasn't for you!"

"You'd have left him sooner or later. I just gave you a little encouragement."

"You've done more than that. Please, Pol! There's far too much for me to even think of handling. Please. I really want to share it with you."

They argued for a long time, Margaret verging on the edge of tears, till finally they reached an agreement. Pauline, her resistance worn down by her friend's insistence said she would accept five of the coins.

"Ten!" said Margaret. "That still leaves me with one hundred and ninety. What the hell am I going to do with all that? I'm beginning to wish we had never found it!" The tears were starting. Pauline gave in.

"Alright then, ten but that's an end to it, Marg. I don't want us to quarrel, especially over money – our friendship is worth more than that."

With that sorted, now all Margaret had to do was run the gauntlet of gossip and face the music of a failed marriage.

CHAPTER 22

A Fresh Start

IT WAS WONDERFUL to be back home, welcomed with open arms into the bosom of her family again, all her worries starting to shrink as she shared them. There had only been one problem during her revelations to them all – the reactions of her father and her brother Brian. They had wanted to flush Godfrey out there and then knock the living daylights out of him. It had taken all her and her mother's powers of persuasion to leave things be, keep their dignity and not make things any the worse for her. Finally they had grudgingly promised to do so. She hoped she could believe them.

The following day she turned up at the Cop a little earlier than usual. Partly to avoid the company of early customers on their way down there and partly to see Mr Williams on his own: before the rest of the staff turned up. She wanted to sort out a week's holiday and inform him of the reason for it – that she needed time on her own away from everything to come to terms with the break-up. He understood and sympathised immediately. He put his arm around her shoulder.

"And about time, too, Maggs. You've done the right thing. You leave it to me." He knew all about Godfrey's worsening behaviour as time had gone on.

She told the girls before the shop opened, while they were all in the back room depositing their coats and bags, her declaration blunt; "I've left Godfrey. For good." They rallied round her, smiling, patting her on her back. They too, had heard things, and had put two and two together, coming up with the right answer: that no blame could be laid at her door. Something serious had happened to Margaret way back in April, they had noticed. Ever since then her whole attitude towards Godfrey had changed completely. She rarely spoke of him and should anyone else mention him she quickly changed the subject. They knew things had taken a turn for the worse but didn't know why and had never asked, fair play.

"Don't worry Maggs, we're all behind you. We'll set people straight about things," said Moira.

"You're better off without the likes of him," said Sarah.

"I don't know how you put up with him all these months," said Joan. "I would have given him his marching orders long ago!"

They knew nothing of the affair with Isabel and never would do. That information could only come from Godfrey himself and he was far from proud of that episode and far too frightened of Mr Polinski's threats to ever breathe a word of it! The Polinskis had moved away from Crymceynon now. She was grateful for that. Grateful that she wouldn't bump into them unexpectedly, watch the pregnancy develop, re-live it all whenever she caught a glimpse of them. She was so glad she had called on them to explain about that letter. They had been gracious, sympathetic and very relieved to be told that no-one else knew. They had put the house up for sale the following day. How Margaret had continued to live in that street since that awful time, she didn't know. Her departure would have happened now though, come what may, secret hoard or no. Once she had told Pauline, she was prepared for all and sundry to know.

Nine o'clock. It wouldn't be long now before the news circulated. Everyone who was important to her already knew most of the facts. Pauline would have told her parents, sister, her 'Auntie' Vera and her grandparents. And now the Cop staff were all aware.

Godfrey, obviously, wasn't! There was no sign of him. The shop hadn't opened. Another night spent on the town, then! As customers crossed the road to the Cop to complain to her and enquire as to where he was and how long would he be, she found herself answering quite flippantly with the same words he had thrown at her when she had enquired: that it was his business and nothing to do with her! Her courage and confidence increased as the day wore on.

Around dinner-time, the black MG pulled up outside 15 Fair View. Godfrey jumped out, ran up to the house for a quick bite to eat and left again for the shop. A couple of hours serving should bring in a couple of quid! He needed some money. If he didn't have a good win on something soon he would be in dire straits – he owed quite a bit to some very unpleasant blokes who were determined to get it. It wouldn't be long before they managed to track him down.

There were two customers waiting as he unlocked the shop door.

"Afternoon, ladies! Sorry about this morning – had a bit of business to attend to."

One of them tutted, the other said: "Oh well, better late than never, eh Godfrey?"

He could still charm some of them – he hadn't lost his touch!

Carrie was on her way to the Cop, when she spotted him opening up. Impulsively, she crossed the road and entered shortly after the two women.

"Afternoon, Mrs Thomas. Nice day."

She threw him a derisive look, setting her lips in a straight line, refusing to open them. Godfrey raised his eyebrows thinking, *What's up with that old cow, she's in 'em for some reason?* He ignored her, turning his attention back to the other two, taking their orders. Before going into the back room, he spoke to her again, smiling and with a touch of sarcasm.

"And what can I get for you, Mrs Thomas?"

"Nothing, thank you. I just called in to let you know I shall be taking my custom elsewhere from now on!" She had always hated calling there but went for Margaret's sake. Now it was no longer necessary.

"Now why would you want to do that? I've had a few hiccups, I know, learning to run all this on my own," – it paid to remind people he was still suffering, struggling! "But things are more or less sorted now. Back to normal service."

"Hmph! That's not what I've been hearing!"

The other women threw questioning glances at her, then at each other. Godfrey, seeing them, began to feel a little uneasy.

"Oh, give us a chance, Mrs Thomas, I'm trying hard."

One customer nodded in agreement, the other tutted again. The odds were fifty-fifty he could win this. Mrs Thomas, after all, had been there, had witnessed the 'pain' he had suffered on that fateful Friday!

"Margaret is going to feel very upset about this when I tell her!"

Carrie's lips parted now in a triumphant smile. "Oh no, I don't think she will, somehow. In fact, I know she won't!" She faced the two women totally engrossed in watching this crossfire.

"You see," she explained as she moved towards the door, "She's left him! And not before time in my opinion." With that, she flounced out, slamming the door behind her.

Seconds later, she heard the door slam again. Looking round, she saw the woman who had tutted following suit.

"Good!" said Carrie to herself: "That's that done!"

Godfrey absent-mindedly served the remaining customer who tried, but failed, to get him involved in any conversation.

Margaret had left him? Walked out on him? Why would she do that? There was no need. They were more or less leading separate lives as it was. It suited him. It seemed to work with her, too. She hadn't complained – in fact, she hardly said anything! So why this, why now and why so sudden? She couldn't have found out anything about the Polinski business – Alec had threatened that he would tell her but he couldn't have – she would have confronted him with it. They had moved away now, thank goodness, so it was even less likely to become common knowledge. He had to see her, get to the bottom of this, talk it out, find out exactly what she knew – and deny it! He could do it. He could get round her, promise to change, bring up the past again and put all the blame on that!

It was the row they'd had over starting a family that had brought all this on, he was sure. What was she saying to others about that? He had to see her, talk her round before any more serious damage was done to his reputation and the sooner the better. He would go over to the Cop at closing time, show her how upset he was, beg her if necessary to come home, tell her he couldn't face living there without her. That at least would be the truth. He hated being in that house on his own – it had too many memories to haunt him. Besides, who would keep it clean, do his laundry, fork out for most of the bills and cook for him? He needed her, alright!

Five-thirty and the Cop staff were closing up, Joan and

Sarah hovering by the door waiting for Margaret. Out she came and over he went.

"Maggs, Maggs! Hang on a minute please! Can I have a word?"

The two girls moved protectively towards her, concerned for her welfare.

"It's alright," she told them, "I can handle this. You go, both of you."

Wilfred opened the door. "You OK there, Maggs?"

"Yes, I'm fine. Thank you, Mr Williams."

"This door stays open mind, should you want to come back in."

"No, I'm alright really. Thanks."

Godfrey approached her, a look of utter despair on his face. "What's all this about, Maggs? Leaving me – that's not necessary, is it? We get on alright, don't we? And to hear it from Carrie Thomas of all people! What have you been telling her?"

Margaret hid her grin with her hand – trust Carrie, bless her, to start the ball rolling, getting support for her, making sure people knew the truth about who was to blame for this state of affairs.

"Nothing. I've said nothing." But I know who has, she thought.

"I had no idea you felt like this. Why? All marriages go through some sticky patches, don't they?"

Mm – with some far stickier than others, in her opinion, but she let him carry on.

"No marriage is perfect." (Maybe, but the majority seemed to get pretty close to it as time went by!) "Can't we work something out?"

Her reply was spoken calmly in a low voice: "No, Godfrey,

not anymore. I've had enough. More than enough. Of your selfishness, your moods, your temper, your demands, your thoughtlessness – everything! I want my life back. I want peace of mind."

"But I can change all that, Maggs. It's bound to take time for me to adjust to all that happ…" His face crumpled, his eyes filled on cue.

"And that doesn't work anymore either, Godfrey. I know you couldn't care less about your parents. All you ever cared about was getting your hands on their money. And what for? To waste it all on drink, gambling and womanising!"

"Hey, now that's not true!"

"Oh yes it is! *In vino veritas* – as Pauline would say – the truth comes out in drink. You should have been more careful. See how your sins can find you out?"

"What has she got to do with any of this – Miss Pauline Nosey-Parker?"

Margaret's eyebrows rose innocently. "Nothing. She's just my best friend, a true friend. Other than that – nothing. It's my decision – mine alone. No, it's over, Godfrey, and for good. Get used to it. I'm not coming back. Not after all I've found out. Bye!"

With her head held high, she walked away leaving him standing helpless, behind her.

What had she found out? What could he have let slip when he was drunk? Nothing incriminating, he was certain. He was used to handling his drinking since his army days, he knew how to control its effect. She couldn't possibly have found out about Isabel. No-one knew about that except the Polinskis and himself. As to his parents – she couldn't know how they had met their fate. Nothing untoward had even been considered – they were accidents, well and true, as far as everyone was concerned. Even that old cow, Carrie Thomas couldn't deny that. She had been there, after all, had seen everything herself. So Margaret and the rest of them could think what they liked – there was nothing they could pin on him! As to his parents – maybe he had criticised them in front of her once or twice, but who didn't pick faults with their parents on occasion? No, he was positive she could know nothing concrete about anything.

He'd have another go at her. Soon – put it all down to vicious rumour, gossip, even jealousy of some people! Trouble-makers – there were always some in every community!

That evening, he called up to Stephen's Street determined to have another shot. His face fell and he was more than a little taken aback when Brian answered his knock. He was fully expecting it to be Margaret. Still, at least it wasn't her father.

Meekly he asked, with wet eyes and quivering chin: "Hi, Bri. Could I speak to Maggs please? We've had our first big row and I want to set things straight. I want her to come home..."

Brian was looking at him with disgust. "So, you're a bloody liar as well as a bloody wimp!"

What had she told them all? Probably she'd put the blame for the breakdown of the marriage on his announcement that he didn't want children. Ah yes, that would be it. Definitely! She had been a bit upset about that!

"Listen, Bri!"

"I'm listening."

"This is all about us starting a family isn't it? She thinks I don't want to. She's wrong, mun. She's wrong. I meant 'yet'. I'm not ready yet. She's misunderstood, jumped to conclusions. We haven't been married that long after all, have we? Of course I want a family. But it's too soon, Bri. I need a bit more time to get over…" He broke off, took out his hanky, wiped his face and blew his nose. "Sorry, boy. I'm in a hell of a state, I know. I miss her. I need her to come home. Tell her to come to the door, please."

Brian had stood there with his arms folded across his chest and his tongue in his cheek during this sad tale of woe. As Godfrey drew to a close, Brian brought his hands together and slowly applauded.

"That was a bloody good performance Godfrey! You've missed your vocation, boy. You should be on the bloody stage!"

Carelessly, Godfrey allowed the mask of misery to slip and reveal one of seething anger at Brian's sarcasm. It took every once of his willpower not to lash out in temper. Brian, the shorter of the two by a few inches, but standing on the doorstep, stared defiantly into Godfrey's face. He was more than a match for this excuse for a man. He stopped clapping, leaned forward and grabbed his tie, pulling him towards him till his face was within inches of his own. Godfrey's knees sagged under him.

"Now you listen and listen hard, you worthless piece of scum! You have been seen with your pals and your glamour-pussies by people who don't tell lies. You've been seen going in and out of the bookies, handing over large sums and you've been seen getting in to that posh car of yours hardly able to put one foot in front of the other, let alone drive!"

He tightened his grip on the tie. Godfrey gasped for breath.

"You come anywhere near our Margaret ever again and I'll have you mate, I'll bloody have you!"

Brian gave a shove as he let go of his hold. Godfrey stumbled and fell backwards onto his behind. He quickly scrambled to his feet and fumbled with the gate latch before making his escape. Not that Brian intended chasing after him. That little lesson would suffice for now. Brian went in and closed the door. He didn't mention Godfrey's visit to Margaret.

CHAPTER 23

An Up-turn

THE FIRST DAY of Margaret's ordeal – facing everyone at the Cop – had passed surprisingly easily. She felt the worst was over, the only way was up from now on. Pauline called over to see how it went.

"Much better than I had hoped or expected, Pol. He came across from the shop just as we were closing, full of a sob story and apology. That's what I had been dreading most of all – having to face him. I thought I would be scared but I surprised myself – I was as cool as a cucumber! Oh, I'm over him, Pol, well and truly now. There's nothing left now. No feeling for him whatsoever: no love, no hate or even sorrow – nothing."

"Good. I'm glad to hear it."

"Oh, and Mr Williams says I can have the whole of next week off!"

"Oh, that's great, because I've got some good news too! I rang the flat earlier to see if it was alright for you to stay for a few days and guess what? Lucy and Brenda – the two I share with – are both going home to their respective parents' on Friday night and won't be back until the Sunday after next. We can spend the whole week there and take our time getting everything sorted and still have time to go to the theatre, the castle, the museum, the park – oh, and not forgetting shopping, at all the big stores! We'll have a great time."

Margaret, delighted at the prospect, rubbed her hands

together. "Oo, yes, I'd love to! Oo, that sounds marvellous, Pol. A proper holiday for the first time in my life. Oh, I'm really looking forward to that!"

"Good, so am I. If you go to work dressed ready on Saturday, we can catch the one-thirty train. My Dad will bring me and our suitcases down to the Cop in his van, pick you up and we'll be in Cardiff before three. He says he'll pick us up from the flat to come home, seeing as it's on a Sunday. Brenda says you can have her room while she's away – so long as you don't mind the mess and wash her sheets for her – crafty thing! She's not domesticated is our Brend. So what do you say? Saturday afternoon suit you?"

"I say yes! I don't want to waste a second. The thought of all this to come will keep me going for the rest of the week."

"We'll spend the rest of Saturday afternoon going round the shops. You are going to treat yourself, spend a bit on yourself for the first time in years. Marks and Spencer's, British Home Stores, Littlewoods, David Morgan's – eh?"

Margaret beamed.

"Cardiff, here we come!" they said in unison.

So, Saturday dinner-time, Pauline and her father, Jim, pulled up in the van, by the Cop door. In the back were the two suitcases the girls had packed the previous evening, and a holdall containing clean bedding. Jim took them straight to the station carrying both suitcases onto the platform for them. The train arrived within minutes. He kissed them both and waved them off. "You two make the most of this break now. That's an order!"

"Thanks, Dad."

"Thanks, Mr Edwards."

They sat by the window, facing each other, their handbags on their laps. Both opened them simultaneously, both took out their purses and removed a five pound note each.

"My father gave me this and said to share it between us," said Margaret holding it up.

"Snap!" said Pauline, holding up hers.

They burst out laughing at their like-minded fathers, their eyes moistening and shining at their generosity. It set the mood for the whole weekend. They were glad of the extra cash. None of the secret hoard could be spent yet. Not in coin form, hardly.

"Imagine," said Pauline, "going up to the till handing over a sovereign and saying, 'Take it out of that please'!" They had only brought half of the hoard with them, the other half left secreted in Pauline's 'school' bag. No-one would dream of going in there for anything.

After depositing their luggage at the flat, they returned to town and spent the whole of the rest of the day indulging themselves. Lunch upstairs at British Home Stores to begin with, then a browse downstairs to look through the clothes department and to pick up some provisions for the weekend: smoked bacon, cheese, eggs and some of the delicious cream cakes. BHS couldn't be beaten on those items, said Pol. They didn't return to the flat until after closing time, both girls laden with bags. Their last call, on the way home, was to a fish and chip shop for their suppers, wrapped securely in newspaper.

Back at the flat, tired but happy, they transferred their meal onto plates and while those warmed up again in the oven, opened and examined all their purchases and stripped and re-made Brenda's bed. Then, feet up on the couch, the telly switched on, their suppers on their laps, they relaxed for the rest of the evening.

Sunday morning was spent tidying and cleaning the flat. It didn't take long. For lunch they made some bacon sandwiches and ate two of the cakes – each – with a cup of tea, then decided to go out for a walk, just in the immediate vicinity to get some fresh air and exercise. They strolled down the wide street away from the city into a quieter area, entering a tree-lined avenue.

"Oh, this is nice," said Pauline, standing still to take in the view.

Margaret was looking around too, at the houses, semi-detached and much the same design as the ones in Fair View, a bit smaller perhaps but, oh, so much cleaner and brighter looking without the thin layer of coal dust that settled on every surface in the village. The little front gardens, all tidy and cared for, were edged by a low stone wall topped with Victorian styled iron railings, with a gate to match. The only steps to the houses were the front door steps. The paintwork on the iron and the doors and windows all looked fresh and clean.

"Oh, what a lovely street, Pol. Oh, I would love to live somewhere like this – wouldn't you? And with everything you could possibly want almost on your doorstep. I'm falling in love with Cardiff, the more I see of it."

"Mm, yes, I could be very happy living in a street like this. Chance would be a fine thing though, eh?"

They walked a little further when Margaret suddenly stopped dead in her tracks. Pauline turned to her curiously. She was pointing to a house on the other side, her face all lit up.

"Look, Pol, look!" Pauline looked. The house she

was pointing at had a rambling rose, heavily laden with buttercup-yellow blooms, growing on a trellis that was fixed right around the front door.

"Oh, isn't that gorgeous!" she said.

"Not the rose bush. Look there!" In the garden was a 'for sale' sign. They turned to face each other, their faces full of excitement.

"Shall we? Take that chance?"

"Well, I can't see any harm in just making enquiries, Marg."

They crossed the road, opened the gate and rang the bell. An elderly man, neat and clean and leaning heavily on a walking stick, answered. Pauline liked him on sight. Though he must have been several years older than her grandfather, there was a similarity there. Margaret enquired rather tentatively about the sign and both were invited inside. The old man showed them right through the premises, chatting as he went. He was selling up, he said, to move to his daughter's farm in Gloucester. He was a little loath to go – he had lived here all his married life and had been very happy here but his health was failing now, he could no longer manage on his own. His daughter came to see him once a fortnight to do what she could for him: clean through, restock his cupboards, wash and iron but they had a big farm to run and a young family to care for, so it would be best all round if he moved in with them, there. He was resigned to it now and perfectly content with this decision. Besides, he'd get to see a lot more of his grandchildren.

They began the tour upstairs. There were three fair-sized bedrooms, each tastefully decorated and furnished and a small, tiled bathroom. Downstairs was a large front room, a square dining room and a small but functionally set out kitchen. The house, he explained, had to be sold as it stood, all furniture and fittings – apart from personal favourites and items – to be included in the price. His family couldn't afford the time it would take to dispose of everything separately. The 'for sale' sign had only been put up the day before. He hadn't expected any enquiries so soon.

"Well, are you interested? Do you like what you've seen?"

"I love it! I love everything about it. It's perfect!"

"Yes, I can see you do, but can you afford the price? I'm afraid I can't reduce it. But it is a bargain really – all the furniture is good quality. That's if you don't mind it being second-hand."

Margaret nodded in answer to his question. "Yes, I've been lucky enough to inherit some money recently, enough to cover the asking price."

"Right, then. If you can call again on the second Saturday from now, when my daughter and son-in-law will be here, we can start the ball rolling."

They shook hands on it and left.

Back on the street, the girls could hardly contain their excitement. "I've done it Pol! I've bought my dream house! Well, hopefully I will over the next month or so. Oh I do hope nothing goes wrong now! I've set my heart on it!"

"What could go wrong? Things are looking up, Marg. Enjoy it, for goodness sake!" she said, pretending to scold and putting her arm around her shoulder, "You're a funny one, Marg. Once you make your mind up about something there's no stopping you, is there?"

The moment she uttered the words, she regretted them. Margaret came to a dead halt. The words had transported them both back in time to the morning of her wedding when she had made up her mind about marrying Godfrey. Margaret's face had changed from happiness to misery in a split second. She looked mournfully at her friend's face, searching it.

"Do you think I'll live to regret this too, Pol?" She was nervous, serious, all exhilaration gone. "I shouldn't have done it, should I? I should have waited, thought about it. When will I learn?"

Pauline was quick to reassure her. "Nonsense, Marg! I think it's the wisest decision you have ever made. Chances like this don't come along often. You have to grab them when they do. Things will all work out, you'll see."

"But what do I want with a house in Cardiff? It's ridiculous. I live and work in Crymceynon. And how do I explain it to people? I can't mention those coins can I, ever? Not without giving myself away. I'm a thief, aren't I? Whichever way I look at it. It isn't my money. I'm a thief. Oh, what a mess!"

They had reached the flat. Pauline marched her inside and sat her down. She was cross – more than cross – with her friend.

"Now listen to me Margaret. Let's get a few things sorted out here. First, you are not a thief. We have already been over all that so wipe that thought from your mind once and for all. Secondly, none of this is your fault. You married Godfrey, seeing only what he wanted you to see about him. You were deceived from the beginning. You know that now, you can see it for yourself. Thirdly, you did not deserve any of it. Everyone who knows you, loves you. You have the same nature as your mother and you must know how highly she is thought of. Godfrey is the only one who has ever run her down and who values his opinion?"

Ah! Those words hit a nerve, forced a response. Margaret's

lips tightened, her eyes narrowed as she recalled his insulting reference to her beloved Mam.

Pauline carried on: "For a start, no-one need know anything about the house. I could move in, if you'd let me. I've been thinking of getting a place of my own now that I've got a secure job. Everyone will think I'm renting it. And what about you getting a job in Cardiff? You said you'd like to live here, so apply for one. You've seen the huge Co-op that's here, all those departments it's got. Surely there's a vacancy in there somewhere. Mr Williams would find out for you and I'm sure he'd give you a damn good reference!"

She could see Margaret was getting interested now. She pegged away at her persuasion: "It would be worth asking him, Marg. What have you got to lose? Your luck is changing, girl – welcome it with open arms and help it on its way!"

The next few weeks couldn't pass quickly enough for the two girls. They wanted everything signed, sealed and delivered before they could actually believe what they had done. No-one else would be any the wiser for a good while yet as to what they had planned. They would have to be very careful about what they said – one small slip and the cat would be out of the bag! Godfrey would only have to suspect that Margaret had any money of her own and he would be bound to conclude that it must be his, somehow or other.

CHAPTER 24

A Down Turn

TIMES WERE GETTING harder for Godfrey. He had lived on his own now for more than two months. He hadn't slept much during that time. He hadn't been to bed at all, preferring to sleep in an armchair in the kitchen with the light left on all night. Once night fell he couldn't bear to climb the stairs and pass his parents' bedroom door, even though it was kept tightly shut – there were noises in there, there were noises everywhere – the whole house seemed to moan and creak in the early hours. He had never noticed it before, not with Margaret there for company. Now, the slightest sound would have him jumping awake.

All the downstairs rooms were starting to resemble a rubbish tip. Ashes spilled out from fireplaces, dirty clothes littered the furniture, old newspapers cluttered the floor around his chair and the sink and draining board were piled high with dirty dishes. *God, your life is a bloody mess*, he told himself, surveying his surroundings from the armchair. It wasn't supposed to turn out like this. He had almost given up on the shop now. It wasn't worth the bother of opening up. There were fewer and fewer customers. Only last week he had heard one of them saying – loud enough for him and others to hear: "This whole place and 'im are beginning to smell! I'm off. I won't be coming here again. I can't stomach it!" Well, good riddance to him and all the rest of 'em. This was all Margaret's bloody fault. There was nothing he could do about her – she had buggered off somewhere and no-one would tell him where.

All he had left now was his beloved car. He wouldn't give that up without a fight! Trouble was it cost money to run. He sighed, rose from the chair and started picking up some underclothes and shirts, looking for the cleanest to give them a swill through. He had no idea how that contraption of a washing machine worked. He had no idea how to do hand-washing either. Engulfed in a wave of depression he sat down again, the clothes he had chosen lying in his lap. He missed her, that wife of his. He never thought he would. It was what he had intended should happen when he first married her – for them to split up – but these months without her had been hell. His eyes started to genuinely fill up, even though they were tears of self-pity, spilling over his lower lids and running down his cheeks into the creases around his nose and mouth. He wiped them away with the dirty pants, feeling very sorry for himself. He had to get her back. That was the answer, the only answer, to all his problems. She would soon sort everything and he would be able to sleep in his bed again when she was there to keep him company. He knew she was in Cardiff somewhere. He'd fill his car with petrol and drive around until he found her.

Now then, cash! He needed cash. Where could he get some? He searched around looking for something he could sell, opening cupboards and drawers. Ah! Hidden in a dish in the top cupboard of the dresser he found his father's precious gold Hunter watch with its gold chain and albert. His mother had bought it for him on their first wedding anniversary. Well, he wouldn't be needing it where he had gone and Godfrey preferred the one he had bought for himself, a modern one, top of the range, once he'd got his hands on the money. Anyway, you had to wear a waistcoat to show it off properly and who wore bloody waistcoats these days? He wondered if Dudley would be interested in buying it? He'd give him a ring and ask him to call down. If he wasn't interested then he would pawn the damn thing.

Dudley answered and said he'd take a look at it, but not to bank on it. It all depended on what he was asking for it. He'd call down in about an hour's time.

Meanwhile, Godfrey swilled through a change of clothes: one pair of pants, one vest, one shirt and one pair of socks – all dumped in the same bowl of tepid water and each item treated to a smear of toilet soap. He wrung them out and laid them on the fireguard around the fire to drip and dry.

The doorbell rang.

"Ah, come in Dud, through to the kitchen."

Dudley walked behind him down the passage, glancing through the open doors of the other rooms on the way.

"Good God, man!" he exclaimed as they entered the kitchen, "Look at all this bloody mess! How can you live like this? You need to pull your finger out, you lazy sod!"

Godfrey put his finger on his nose and tapped it. "I'll soon get this lot sorted, Dud. I'm off to Cardiff later. I'm going to fetch her back. I won't take no for an answer this time."

Dudley snorted. "You'll be lucky, mate!"

"You wait and see. I'm going to drive around until I find her and work my magic on her!" He tapped his nose again.

He was dwelling in the realms of fantasy now, poor bugger, thought Dudley, chuckling under his breath.

"I can help you there, boy. I know where she lives!" Dudley liked to stir things and stand back to watch the result.

This bloody fine-weather friend of his knew and hadn't said? "You know her address? How long have you known?"

"Not long, mun, don't panic, I was going to tell you anyway. My mother got it from one of her customers who knows the Edwards family. They were saying how well their

Pauline was doing, teaching in Cardiff. She and Margaret rent a house there. It's got roses round the door, apparently – women, huh! – roses round the door!"

Godfrey handed him a pad and biro. "Write it down," he said, jabbing at the pad with his forefinger.

"OK, mun, OK!" He scribbled the address and said "Now where's this watch you were on about?"

"Here it is." He laid it on the table. "What do you think? That's a Hunter watch, mind – it's worth a good bit. It's all solid gold – the watch, the chain and the albert. See for yourself. What's your offer?"

Dudley examined it thoroughly, looking for the hallmarks on each piece and raising his eyebrows approvingly (but not showing Godfrey) when he found them.

"More to the point, how much are you asking?"

"Fifty quid?"

"Whaw, you must be joking!"

"It's worth that and more. You know it is."

"Not to me, it isn't."

"OK, as I'm a bit strapped for cash at the moment, I'll take forty-five."

"You're always strapped for bloody cash these days!" *And no fun to be with anymore,* thought Dudley.

Godfrey was thinking: *Aye, that's why I never see you these days unless I have some winnings to spend.*

"Thirty I'm offering. Take it or leave it." He had to have money. Dudley knew it.

"OK, make it thirty-five, Dud, and it's yours!"

"You drive a hard bargain, boy. Alright, thirty-five quid it is!" He took out a roll of notes and peeled some off. "Though why I'm buying it, I don't know! It's not the sort of thing you can wear nowadays, is it?"

I'm a damned good liar, thought Dudley, smiling to himself again. *And Godfrey Parson is a bloody idiot!* He made a quick departure with the watch tucked safely in his pocket.

Chapter 25

You Reap What You Sow

Godfrey washed and shaved at the kitchen sink, dressed in the still slightly damp underclothes and partially-ironed shirt and stood before the dresser mirror surveying the result. He didn't look too bad, the collar wasn't creased that much. He ran a comb through his hair, put on his jacket and trilby and left the house. Sitting behind the wheel of the car he switched on and let the feeling of power sweep over him as it always did when the engine roared. The first port of call was the petrol station to fill her right up while he still had money in his pocket. He had to keep her going – he would be lost without her. The job done, he was off to Cardiff.

Once there, he bought a small bunch of flowers from a barrow boy and made enquiries as to where to find the address Dudley had given him. He soon found the place, parked at the end of the avenue and waited for Margaret to come home from work. Shops closed at five-thirty. It was coming up to five-fifty now. The November weather was living up to its reputation – dark, dismal, dreary and drizzling. Ah! There she was, holding up an umbrella over her face but he'd recognise that figure and quick walk of hers anywhere. By damn, she was looking smart! He knew quality clothes when he saw them. She must be doing alright for herself.

He got out and approached her, his trilby pulled well down over his forehead. She didn't notice him until he stopped in front of her.

"Hello, Margaret."

She froze with terror. "Godfrey!"

"Yes, it's me." He offered her the flowers. "I, er, I've bought you these."

She felt like laughing out hysterically but fought hard against it and won. The farcical side of his gesture restored her confidence, dispersing her fear. She looked at his sorry bunch of blooms but made no move to take them.

"I know you love flowers."

Well, she would never have guessed that he knew! What was he after now? With the patience of Job heavily in her tone of voice she asked: "What do you want, Godfrey?"

She had the upper hand in this situation – she felt it. She would make him sweat for a change. He was just a shadow of his former self now, nothing to fear anymore.

"You, Maggs! That's what I want! Come back home, please, I'm begging you. Look!"

He actually went down on one knee before her! He would do whatever it took. He looked up at her, trying to invoke her pity.

"I miss you so much, Maggs. It's the truth – just look at me! Look at the state I'm in!"

She was finding it harder to control that laughter bubbling inside her. He'd been drinking, obviously.

"You look ridiculous! Get up for goodness sake, Godfrey!"

He saw the corners of her lips twitch with a hovering smile and jumped to the wrong conclusion. He was getting there!

"Can I come in? Can we talk?" Coaxing now, like a naughty boy trying to get back in his mother's good books.

"You must be joking. Certainly not. Just get it through

your thick skull, Godfrey. It is over. I wish I had never set eyes on you. I wouldn't live with you again if you were the last man on earth!"

Crestfallen, he rose to his feet again. He could see it was no use. She wasn't having any of it.

"Alright, I'll go. I won't bother you again."

He offered the flowers once more. She looked up at the sky – anywhere but at his face – and was losing patience with him, fast.

"Could you do me one last little favour, Maggs?"

She closed her eyes – she knew what he wanted – then opened them enquiringly but didn't speak.

"You couldn't lend us a couple of quid, could you? I've come out without my wallet."

"Hah!" she said again to the sky above her. "And where do you think I've got money from, Godfrey? You never gave me any, did you?"

He was getting angry with her now, with this attitude of hers. Damn her! His voice changed from whining to aggression.

"Well, you must be doing alright, affording rent on a house like this. You and Pauline got yourselves a sugar-daddy each or what?"

She slapped him hard across his face. "How dare you speak to me like that. How dare you!"

With no hesitation he threw a punch back at her just as she was about to turn and walk away from him. It caught her on the side of her face with a force that knocked her to the ground. He bent over, snarling at her.

"You tight-fisted bitch! You're worse than my bloody parents were. You deserve to get what they got!"

She screamed as he lifted his fist again. The door of the

house next door opened, a big man and a dog appearing in the frame, about to take a short stroll.

"Hey! What the hell is going on out here?"

He got quickly to his gate. Godfrey fled back to his car, got in and sped off. The neighbour went to Margaret's aid.

"Are you alright, miss?" She managed to stand with his help. "What was that all about? Who was he?"

"I don't know," she said, holding her head and shaking it slowly. "He said he wanted money."

"Did he get any?"

"No."

The neighbour escorted her to her own front door, telling Pauline, when she answered his knock, all he had seen and heard.

"Shall I ring the police for you?"

"No," said both women together.

"There's really no need," said Margaret, "I was just unlucky, I suppose. In the wrong place at the wrong time. I think he just saw an opportunity and took it, on the spur of the moment. He seemed desperate for money and was stinking of drink."

"Are you sure you are alright? Perhaps we should ring them."

"No, I'm fine now, really. I don't want any bother."

"Well, if you're sure…" He gave a little whistle to his dog to come to his side.

"Thanks for what you did," said Pauline, making a subtle move to see him out. "I'll see to her. She'll be alright."

"Nothing like this has ever happened round here before," said the man as they reached the door. "What is the world coming to, I ask myself!"

Pauline agreed she didn't know, either. "Thanks again for your help. Goodnight."

Back in the living room, Pauline looked at the damage to Margaret's face, wincing at the thought of the force Godfrey must have used.

"Stay there, don't move. I'll get the witch-hazel and something to ease the pain."

She returned with the first-aid box, a tea-towel and a small packet of frozen peas from the freezing compartment in the fridge. She soaked a piece of cotton wool with the witch-hazel, placed it on the bruise and lifted Margaret's hand to hold it there while she wrapped the peas in the tea-towel and placed them on top.

"The bruise should be out by the morning. You're going to have a beauty of a black eye!"

"This is a fine start for me in my new job, isn't it? I haven't been there five minutes. I can't take time off for this. What is everyone going to think, Pol? What will I say?"

"That you walked into a door, of course! It's not always domestic violence!" She wanted confirmation: "It was this time though, wasn't it? It was Godfrey, wasn't it?"

"Yes."

"I thought so. When our neighbour brought you in he handed me your bag and a bunch of flowers. He thought you had dropped them. I knew you hadn't because we only bought some yesterday. Best to leave him think that. That's why I brought them in." She sat down beside her friend. "Now tell me, Marg. I want to hear every single word he said, every detail of what happened."

When she repeated what Godfrey had said about his parents and the threat he had made to her, she got up again, abruptly.

"Where are you going?"

"To ring your Brian!"

"No, Pol, don't! I don't want our Brian getting into any trouble."

"Your Brian is not daft, Marg. Far from it. He'll give him a damn good pasting to remember, put the fear of God in him, that's all. This is not going to happen again!"

Godfrey, driving back to Crymceynon, stopped the car near a pub. He needed a drink. He was still shaking – partly with anger, mostly with fear. He tried to remember exactly what he had said to Margaret about his parents' 'accidents'. Enough for her to realise what he had done? Would she do anything about it, if she did? Tell anyone? That nosey bitch of a friend of hers, for instance? If she did, it was too late to shut them both up now. They'd be on the phone to the police with their theories! He couldn't go through all that questioning again and put on a convincing performance. He searched through his pockets. He still had a couple of quid left. A drink would help him to think clearly. He walked into the pub, bought a pint and a small bottle of whisky, downed the beer and got back in the car, taking a few swigs from the bottle before starting off.

Brian Pierce sat astride his motorbike not far from 15 Fair View. It was pitch dark now but his lights were switched off. A car passed him – an MG – there weren't many of those in Crymceynon! It was him. It pulled up outside number fifteen, the door opened and Godfrey got out. He turned unsteadily to close the car door and began the walk towards his gate. Brian switched on his headlamp, the full beam falling full on him.

"Hang on a minute, Godfrey! I'd like a word with you!"

He recognised the voice, turned and hurried back to his

car. Brian bided his time, waiting for him to turn on the ignition and pull away from the kerb. Then he revved his bike and followed at a reasonable distance. It was obvious that Godfrey was the worse for drink – it would be unwise to get too close. Godfrey, seeing the wide gap, thought the car could easily outrun the bike so he, too, kept a steady pace through the streets. Once out of the village and onto the Bwlch road he would leave Brian far behind. He couldn't see what kind of bike he had but it couldn't be much good. That family didn't have money to throw around – they couldn't have – not with a brood of that size to feed!

He was wrong. Brian had worked and saved hard for years. If you wanted a thing badly enough, you were prepared to make sacrifices to get it and Brian had always wanted a motorbike, a good one. It was a Triumph Twin. It could shift alright!

They left the village behind them, heading for the mountain road that connected the valleys. Brian increased his speed now, closing the gap between them and turned on his full beam. It hit onto Godfrey's driving mirror, dazzling him and he put his foot down in an effort to get away from it. Brian kept up with him, completely in control of his vehicle and conscious of the layout of the road. Godfrey, blinded by the beam, hazy with alcohol, terrified as to Brian's intentions if and when he'd be forced to stop, was driving like a man possessed.

A hairpin bend was coming up. Brian, knowing the road like the back of his hand, cut his speed, widening the gap again. Godfrey, able to look in his mirror again, thought he was out-running his pursuer at last and kept up his pace. He lost control right on the bend, the MG shooting over the edge and into the air, somersaulting and landing with a tremendous bang before rolling down the mountainside to the bottom.

Brian came to a stop on the grass verge of the bend just as the vehicle burst into flames. Slowly, he turned his bike, wheeled it back onto the road and made his way back to the village, stopping at the first telephone kiosk he came to. He made two phone calls. One to the police to report a nasty accident on the Bwlch road, putting the phone back on its hook before questions were asked, and one to Cardiff.

"It's over, Pol. No more trouble from that source. An accident, pure and simple."

An account appeared in the local newspaper a few days later: "Local butcher Mr Godfrey Parson of Fair View, Lower Crymceynon, was killed in a car accident on the Bwlch road. A whisky bottle was recovered at the scene. It is believed the MG he was driving took the hairpin bend at high speed. Mr Godfrey Parson was the third and last member of his family to die from a tragic accident, all three occurring within the last three years. No-one else was involved."

Brian cut it out and posted it to Margaret.

Only two people attended Godfrey's funeral: Margaret, his only surviving relative, and Pauline, there to support her friend. What was left of the body was cremated. On receiving notification that the urn was ready to collect, both women travelled to Crymceynon with it and walked up the mountain behind Stephen's Street. Reaching the summit, they walked over towards Lower Crymceynon and stood on the edge of the quarry there. Margaret removed the urn's lid and passed it to Pauline. Moving closer to the edge, she held the urn out at arm's length.

"Well, you always wanted the high life, God. Too bad

you never made it. Still, I suppose a high death is the next best thing, eh?"

She turned the urn over and tipped out its contents.

"Trouble is, the higher you climb, treading on others to get there, the further you fall."

The ashes floated on the breeze, drifting downwards.

"And you hit rock bottom before you know it!"

She dropped the urn and watched it smash to smithereens on the rocks below.

Brian was waiting for them at the foot of the mountain. When Margaret spotted him, she ran up to him and wrapped her arms around him tightly, her emotions high-pitched with relief.

"Thanks, Bri!"

"What for? I haven't done anything."

"Oh yes, you have! You've given me back my peace of mind at last." She turned to her friend. "And you, Pol, with that phone call you made."

"I knew it was the right thing to do, Marg. I knew Brian would handle things and wouldn't do anything foolish."

"Of course I wouldn't. No, it all worked out well. I just followed him and waited for him to run out of petrol or something. It was his own fault – driving at that speed and as drunk as a newt. I knew as we came up to the bend that he would over-shoot it."

He diverted his eyes as guilt suddenly cast a shadow over them and continued in a quiet voice, still looking down: "Perhaps I did contribute to it – chasing him like I did."

"Nonsense!" said both girls.

Brian, a puzzled look on his face now, lifted his head and stared ahead. "I've been thinking," he said, "Perhaps he wanted that to happen. His life hasn't exactly been worth living these last couple of months, has it? It could be that he wanted to end it all!"

The irony of what he had just said didn't escape him.

"He has ended up in exactly the same situation as his parents, hasn't he? With us three still wondering whether they died by accident, suicide or murder and exactly the same questions applying to him."

"Oh, he murdered them, I'm sure of it," said Margaret, "but I don't see how he could have done it. It baffles me."

"Whatever the cause of his or their deaths, one thing's for sure. He bloody-well deserved what he got, unlike his poor parents!"

CHAPTER 26

The Start of Something?

CHRISTMAS IN A few days' time. The children's department at the Cardiff Co-op was heaving with customers and Margaret was rushed off her feet. But she was enjoying it, happier than she had been for a very long time. From the corner of her eye she had noticed a man hovering for a while over a display of children's bedroom slippers. He obviously couldn't decide which ones to buy. When she finished serving her customer she walked over to him.

"Do you need any help, sir?"

Without looking up he said: "Oh, if you would, please! I'm looking for a pair for my god-daughter. I've got the size and everything. I just can't decide which ones she'd like."

Margaret picked up a pair of pink ones with darker pink satin bows and held them out to him.

"These are very popular."

He took them from her and was about to thank her, when he recognised who she was.

"Good gracious! Margaret Pierce!"

"Michael Richards! Gosh, I haven't seen you for years? How are you?"

"I'm fine. You look well. What are you doing here?"

"Um, I work here, Michael."

"Of course you do! Silly me. Heck, it must be all of ten, twelve years, since I saw you last. You haven't changed a bit. How long have you been working here? Do you live near or travel in?"

People were waiting to be served and getting a little impatient. She motioned to him that she had to get on, whispering as she gave him his change.

"It's great seeing you, Mike, but I really can't stop." She indicated the queue with a sweep of her arm. "You can see how busy it is and the supervisor is hovering over there."

"Oh, of course. Sorry, Marg, sorry." He picked up his parcel. "Can we meet lunchtime, go for a cup of tea or something?"

"Yes. That would be lovely."

"Right, see you outside, what time?"

"Twelve-thirty?"

They managed to grab two empty seats in a café not far from the store. While Michael joined the queue by the counter, Margaret reminisced to herself about their childhood days. Oh, the hours she and Pauline had spent, sitting on the stile by the Navigation pub, reading their Enid Blyton books. Sooner or later Michael would spot them from one of the windows and come across to join them, climbing up to perch between them. He was quite smitten with Pauline then, and for years afterwards with them both attending the same grammar school and going on to university together. Pol always used to mention him in her letters. She hadn't heard her mention him since. They had both gone their separate ways probably, or someone else may have come on the scene. She wondered if he still carried a torch for her, still fancied her? She'd do her best to find out.

Michael returned with their coffees. "Half your lunch hour's gone already waiting for these! Sorry about that."

"It's not your fault, is it?" she smiled. "It's like a fair everywhere today. Are you staying in Cardiff? Do you live here?"

"Yes, as from this week. I'm lodging with a mate of mine till I find a place of my own. I work here now."

"What do you do? You were going in for architecture, weren't you? So Pauline said."

"Yes that's right. I work for Cardiff Council now, so does Pete Hawkins, the man I'm lodging with." There was a slight pause. "Er, do you keep in touch with Pauline Edwards at all? I know you two were always very close pals."

He was still interested then – she could read it in his expression and hesitation.

"Funny you should ask that!" she replied. Her smile was almost splitting her face. She's lodging with me at the moment, until she finds a place of her own!"

"Well I never! She's not married then?"

"Nope."

"Is she, er, seeing anyone do you know?"

"Nope." Margaret was enjoying this. The delight on his face was a picture. Impulsively, she said "Why don't you and er, Peter, was it? Why don't both of you come round tonight? I know she would love to see you again."

He jumped at the chance but tried hard not to sound too eager.

"Would that be OK, do you think?"

Believe me, thought Margaret, *that will be fine!* She couldn't wait.

"We haven't made any other arrangements, as far as I know. It's the last few days of term, so she won't be bringing any urgent work home to do."

Michael leaned back. "That's great! Perhaps the four of us could go out somewhere, make a night of it? What do you think?"

"Fine, or we could stay in and chat – we can decide on

that later." She wrote her address quickly on a serviette and handed it to him. "I'd better be getting back. See you around seven-thirty then, OK? Here's my address. It's not hard to find."

"Yeah, thanks, Maggs. It's been great meeting up with you again. Give my regards to Pol, won't you?"

Like heck I will, thought Margaret. And spoil this surprise? Now then, how to get Pauline dressed in her 'glad-rags' without telling her why!

*

Pauline, finishing her work, more than an hour before Margaret, had their evening meal ready and waiting. They sat, ate and chatted about the day's events, Margaret omitting to tell her friend about Michael, of course. They washed up and cleared away between them, then settled themselves in the front room. Pauline curled up on the couch with one of her Bronte books. Margaret kept fidgeting and interrupting.

"Oh, let's go out somewhere, Pol: pictures, milk-bar, or just for a walk around looking at window displays, anything! It's a lovely, clear night out there."

"Yeah, OK. We may as well. I can see I'm not going to have any peace to read my book, am I? I'll get my coat."

"No, I feel like dressing up, as if we've got somewhere special to go to. We never know who we'll meet or where we'll end up, do we? Let's dress up a bit and get into the spirit of Christmas. There'll be crowds out there, all going somewhere special and I want to feel part of it."

How could she refuse? It was good to see her friend so happy these days, with a zest for life again.

By seven-twenty, Pauline was ready and waiting for Margaret to put the finishing touches to her hair. With one eye on the clock, Margaret was wondering what else she could do to delay their 'departure'. *Please don't be late Michael*, she whispered to herself. She slipped her shoes off to give them a rub with a duster.

"For goodness sake, Marg, who's going to notice them? It's dark out there and anyway, they're clean enough. If you take much longer the night will be over!"

Saved by the bell!

"Who can that be, this time of the night?"

Margaret shrugged. "I don't know! You answer it, Pol. I'm all but ready now."

Pauline tutted and reached for her purse. "Carol singers, I expect. It's the same nearly every blooming night in the run-up to Christmas back home, isn't it? It's probably the same here!"

Margaret, one shoe on, the other in her hand, hopped down the passage behind her getting there just as the door opened.

"Hiya, Pol!"

"Michael!" They embraced. No, hugged! Off to a good start, then!

Slipping on her other shoe, Margaret moved forward as Peter Hawkins tried to gain access past the clinched couple. She shook his hand, her eyes automatically taking in information as normally happens when meeting someone for the first time. She liked what she saw but nothing about him made any special impact on her. He was a bit taller than herself, a few years older, maybe. An open, honest kind of face, dark hair, a bit unruly and held in place with a touch of Brylcreem. Nice smile, nice teeth, dark brown eyes that looked directly at you when he spoke. She liked that. And he was easy to talk to, she could tell that already, the way he had jerked his head at the other two saying in a whisper: "Old friends, I take it?" accompanied by a knowing wide grin. He was neatly but not expensively dressed; did most of his shopping in Marks probably, or BHS. No colour sense by the look of things – that tie definitely didn't go with that shirt! All in all, what one would call a nice man, was her summing up.

Introductions over and Pol's accusation thrown – "You knew didn't you! You had this planned all along!" – they discussed what to do with the rest of the evening and decided on one of the big cinemas.

Shown to their seats, Margaret manipulated the seating arrangements. Pauline entered first, then stepping aside, she let Michael go next, then her, followed by Peter. The film, *Love Is A Many Splendored Thing* – a sentimental story of forbidden love – starred William Holden, one of the girls' favourites, and was thoroughly enjoyed by all four.

The show over, they walked slowly back to the avenue, separating into couples: Pauline and Michael in front, Margaret and Peter following a few yards behind, talking easily to each other and each learning quite a lot about the other. He was one of a large family – six children in all, three sisters and two brothers, all older than himself and all married. He wasn't. He hadn't found anyone suitable yet, though it wasn't for want of looking! He lived in hope.

"How about you?" He had noticed she didn't wear any rings on her left hand.

"I was married – for about two years."

"Divorced?"

"No. Widowed. He was killed in a car accident a couple of weeks ago."

"Oh, I'm sorry, I'm so sorry! I didn't mean... I shouldn't have asked."

"Don't apologise. It's quite alright. If he hadn't died we would have been divorced. My marriage was a total disaster from the beginning." She paused for a minute or two but decided to tell him. "The main reason, though there were plenty of others, was his refusal to start a family. He didn't want children."

"What? He didn't want children? What a strange thing to say!"

"There would be no children in our marriage ever. He said he didn't want *kids*, wouldn't have *kids* and that was final." Her lips curled as she said the word *kids*.

"I hate that expression – *kids*" said Peter. "It's so disrespectful to children, I think. They are not animals."

Margaret nodded, warming a little towards this kindred spirit. "I was longing for a baby before the first year was over. I thought that after a year he would have changed his mind. I'm one of eleven children, four of them younger than me. There's always been a baby in my life to love. To have my own would have been my ultimate pleasure. But he refused."

Peter was silent. He couldn't intrude on her thoughts at this point. Her head was down. She was reliving it all, he knew.

She lifted her head again. "That's not all," she said brightly, "you haven't heard the best bit. He got another woman pregnant and demanded that she got rid of it! So you see, you hadn't intruded into any grief! I really worshipped that man. I foolishly thought he felt the same. I soon found out differently. I won't make the same mistake again in a hurry!

Anyway, enough of my past. I intend to focus on the future from now on."

The couple in front were singing.

"Listen to those two," she said. "Oh it's been a lovely evening, Peter. I've really enjoyed myself. Let's join in."

They caught up with the couple in front, linked arms and added their voices to the song from the film:

Once, on a high and windy hill
In the morning mist
Two lovers kissed
And the world stood still…

They were all laughing as they tried to remember the words. Peter stole a glance across to Margaret. He was beginning to like this girl who grabbed at happiness, who was determined to enjoy life's simple pleasures. What she must have suffered, being denied her natural desire, all that energy and passion for living and loving clamped down.

They were nearly at her front door. They parted into couples again, this time Pauline and Michael falling behind. Peter put his hand on Margaret's arm, gently restraining her, as she delved into her bag for her keys.

"Margaret?"

She paused, her hand still in her bag and looked up at him. "Mm?"

"Look, um, I've thoroughly enjoyed your company tonight," he took a quick look behind him, "and it's obvious those two have!"

She agreed with a wide grin – mission accomplished, she thought to herself. Peter was struggling to find the right words about something. She turned her attention to him.

"Er, do you think all four of us could repeat it, sometime?"

She surprised herself with her spontaneous response. "Yes, I'd like that. That would be nice." Her voice sounded sincere.

Encouraged, he continued: "Or, perhaps, if those two wanted to go off on their own, we could…?"

She said yes again.

Boldly, he asked "How about tomorrow? It's Sunday, after all – a free day – perhaps we could…?" He left the question hang in mid-air.

Michael and Pauline had reached the gate. They were still singing. The other two joined in again as they all entered the house:

Love is a many splendored thing,
It's the only rose that ever grows in the early spring;
It is nature's way of giving
A reason to be living…

Also by Sheila Morgan:

A humorous war-time story set in the Welsh valleys

olicka bolicka

& Pink Bluebells

Sheila Morgan

y Lolfa

Feet of Clay is a sequel to her first novel *Olicka Bolicka and Pink Bluebells*, set in a south Wales mining village during the Second World War and telling the story of the Edwards family, recently re-located there, and how they cope with their change of environment and the many emotional challenges that are thrown at them.

£7.95